TRUST ME 2

CARTER & AMANI'S STORY CONTINUED

KÄIXO

KAIXO BOOKS PUBLISHING

ALSO BY KÄIXO

Promising My Love to a Boss Series:

Promising My Love to a Boss

Promising My Love to a Boss 2

Promising My Love to a Boss 3

Promising My Love to a Boss 4

Bankroll Boyz Series:

Give Me All of You

Give Me All of You 2

Give Me All of You 3

Carter & Amani [Continuing Series]:

Trust Me

Trust Me 2

Standalone Books:

Rein

And so much more to come!

CONTENTS

Preface	vii
Chapter 1	1
Chapter 2	10
Chapter 3	22
Chapter 4	31
Chapter 5	46
Chapter 6	55
Chapter 7	71
Chapter 8	85
Chapter 9	95
Chapter 10	104
Chapter 11	108
Chapter 12	118
Chapter 13	124
Chapter 14	130
Graduation Day (Epilogue)	137
Amani's Day (Epilogue)	140
About the Author	145

PREFACE

NOT REALLY A CHAPTER BUT INSTRUCTIONS YOU SHOULD FOLLOW TO ENJOY THIS RIDE THROUGH LOVE...

Just like the prequel, there's a playlist you can listen to when you want. You access it here.

But I want to address a reader or few who may have been upset with the way the book read. These are standalone novels (granted its probably best that you read Trust Me 1 before you pick up this book, it's not required for you to read Promising My Love to a Boss Series or Give Me All of You Series. These characters don't have significant parts in those series. And neither do the main characters of those series. Torin probably appears once and Troy the same. But if you'd like to read up, go to the **Also by Käixo** part of the table of contents and download those other books.)

So without further delay... Enjoy your time at home with the sequel to Wild Side!

Whether you're Team Girl or Boy,
Käixo

---

*No smoking this time around... For the baby's sake!

**But you're welcome to pour you a glass because I'm sipping sangria as I type this 😊 .

CHAPTER ONE

Amani

Pushing my shopping cart a half inch further, Ebony was stopping us once again. Pointing and smiling as another gadget caught her eyes. If you couldn't see my stomach protruding like I was hiding a ripe watermelon underneath my shirt, you'd think Ebony was the one pregnant. Since twelve this afternoon, she dragged me out of bed to finish baby shopping. Something I thought we'd finished last week. That's what the two packed rooms, near the unfinished nursery would tell you if they could talk. Carter and I had, well over, the necessary amount of baby clothes, bags, shoes, strollers, car seats, and every damn thing in between. And I do mean damn... Because *damn!* I can't take it anymore.

"Ooo, I like this one!" Ebony gushed as she pulled the electric bouncer from the shelf to place into her cart. "You think I should get da blue one, instead?" she asked, looking over the yellow bouncer inside her cart.

Rounding my eyes as I twisted my lips and shrugged, I didn't have a need for most of the stuff she was tossing into our carts but I didn't put up a fight about it, either. This baby brought more joy to Carter's family and mine, than indigestion. And boy did I hate this acid reflux. Every day and night, my chest burned and Fatima was so sure that was a dead giveaway that I was bringing a hairy boy into the world because she'd gone through the motions three times. To which I'd relay her messages to Carter who'd have a fit, telling me the exact opposite. Whatever I was having... *Hopefully a boy* because I could no longer feel confident telling Carter it was a boy—Since, I'd lost that feeling I once had during my early stages but I wasn't going to call this baby a girl and deal with Carter bragging about how he'd known it since he knocked me up. I already went through that enough when I came home to him touching and rubbing my stomach as he told me, this was bound to happen.

"You be tryna plan shit out but dat ain't how life goes... Ain't dat right baby girl?"

That's what he'd say as he placed his ear to my stomach then laugh once the baby kicked back. What he called *her* way of agreeing with him. As cute as it was, I'd play annoyed and then laugh when Carter nudged me followed by a kiss and some bedroom fun. Because I was always horny. I thought the baby books I'd been reading overexerted just how much sex I'd crave but I might have to rewrite a book or two of my own because my hormones were raging now just thinking about sex.

"Do y'all even know what ya'll havin'?" Ebony's question pulled me from my thoughts as I shook my head, hearing my phone chirping inside my purse.

"We were gonna find out but Carter was so irritating with the constant girl this and girl that..." I sighed as I unzipped my purse. "I just decided it'd be best if we waited for the grand reveal—*Hello?*"

"*Butta Love—*"

"Shut up," I giggled, hearing his chuckles on the other end.

"Whatchu doin' Shawty?"

"Getting some more baby things we won't use—"

"Yes, ya'll is!" Ebony picked up on my sarcasm quickly as I giggled, averting her gaze. "I'll be over there to make sure of it, too!" she told me as Carter laughed.

"It's too much—"

"*You can't neva have too much,*" Carter and Ebony spoke in unison as I groaned.

"You shut up," Carter quickly told me as I smirked. "You ain't neva had a baby before—"

"And you're telling me this why?" I cut him off because I hated when he told me that.

"Cuz you'on know whatchu need—And it's better to have more than enough than just enough... Dat way you can donate whateva we don't use or keep it for da next baby," he tossed that last part in as I rolled my eyes, choosing not to give him the verbal response, I felt he was itching for. "So, you ain't gon' say non—"

"I knew you that's what you wanted!" I cackled with him as Ebony helped pull my cart along so I could push with my free hand and talk on the phone with the other. "We're going to put a two-year difference between the two... I know that much," I stamped my feet as I walked for emphasis. "And *I do* know what I need—First baby and all... It doesn't take experience to know a few diapers, wipes, a crib, and some clothes is just enough," I said, hearing Ebony scoff as Carter did the same in my ear. "You don't even have kids—"

"Who?" Carter was quick to counter my claim.

"Not you, nosey, I'm talking to Ebony."

"Eh—"

"No, you, Eh..." I rolled my eyes, growing tired of rolling through the same four aisles. "I just wanna eat," I whined as Ebony turned back with a grin on her face. "And Ebony is just holding me hostage, here and you're allowing her to—"

"I told you to stay wit me," Carter countered as I exhaled, remembering those exact words when Ebony called five minutes before she was knocking on the front door. "You ain't wanna listen—"

"I heard you but you saw Ebony pull me out of—"

"I ain't pull shit—You came willingly," Ebony was lying through her teeth as my mouth hung open in disbelief. "Besides..." she blew air from mouth. "We almost finished... I saw dis baby bath back in stock and I wanna get it," Ebony's eyes lit up as she pulled the baby-sized tub from the shelves.

It resembled the porcelain tubs in your actual bathroom with a faucet and removable showerhead. Cute, *yes*, but excessive. But of all the baby things I've gotten since confirming my pregnancy, this was probably my favorite.

"I see dat smile!" Ebony caught me ogling over the baby tub as my lips spread across my face. "They gotta toilet, too—When ya'll start potty trainin' I'm gettin' it!" Ebony promised, and I took her word for it.

"Carter?" I called out his name, finding his silence odd.

Pulling my phone from my ear, I was even more surprised to see he'd hung up. Smacking my lips as I dialed his number again, a familiar scent hit my nose just before the blaring of a ringtone I'd heard several times before. Turning on my heels with a smile on my face, Carter was creeping up the aisle with a similar smile on his face. Running his tongue over his lips just as he reached me, I melted the moment his arms wrapped around me. Never feeling safer until he held me, I was the baby in our relationship and Carter didn't mind holding me. All night long, while we were cuddling on the couch, and just anywhere in public. We could be waiting in line, and I'd be enveloped in his arms. He'd changed me from being self-conscious about PDA to expecting a touch, kiss, or some form of playful touching whenever he was near me.

"You miss me?" he mumbled against my lips as I giggled and nodded. "I know," he cockily pecked my lips, removing his hand from the small of my back to grip the back of my neck.

Squeezing briefly, he released my neck looking past me at Ebony as he cut his eyes, causing me and her to laugh.

"Whatchu lookin' at?" he teased as she smacked her lips. "Yo man somewhere—"

"I know..." Ebony smirked just as Collin hit the corner. "He just texted me—"

"Who just texted you?" his voice boomed as I watched Ebony exhale causing me to snicker.

"Who you think?" she asked in sarcasm.

Pulling her into a half hug as he kissed the side of her face, Collin's eyes gave Ebony a once over as the stark look on his face remained. Watching her intently, Ebony cracked up laughing as I looked up his brother to see if he was joking. I'd been around Collin a lot and normally he was sillier than Carter but there were times when I didn't know where he was coming from. He just had that look about him. Like if I hadn't met him through Carter, I'd steer clear of him. Sort of the same way I used to view Torin. They can be assholes when they wanted to be.

"You better stop showin' out in front of yo brotha," Ebony

rolled her eyes as Collin stared her down a second longer then broke into a smile. "Dats what I thought—"

"*Tsk*—Quit playin', Eb," Collin smacked his lips in a huff causing me and Ebony to giggle. "Ain't shit funny—Ya'll out here gettin' all dis bullshit when Carter just gon' hold her all day and night," Collin shook his head disapprovingly as he picked through some things in Ebony's cart. "Ain't ya'll ever heard of waitin' to see how big ya'll baby gon' be before ya'll stock up on pampers?" Collin was giving one of my points I'd ran by Carter multiple times.

Twisting my lips as I looked up at Carter he was already watching me with his eyes low as I doubled over in laughter. Muffing the side of my face, I could see a small smile on his face as I looked back up at him.

"Shut up," he mouthed before I could speak. "I already said what I said," he told me as I remembered how adamant he was about how big the babies in his family are born.

I just let him talk because his excitement moved me to love him all the more. Even if he was wrong, which I'd mentally prepared myself for... Knowing he cared enough to convince himself was just enough.

"We ain't stock up—Mani has four newborn sizes, four size ones and two of the size twos... I've watched—"

"Chupi ain't dis baby," Collin cut Ebony off before she could finish talking. "All babies born different—"

"Why you so worried anyway, bro?" Carter cut in as Collin shook his head, waving his hand back and forth.

"I ain't—"

"Yes, you are!" Ebony giggled as Carter opened his mouth to probably say the same thing. "And it doesn't matter because ya'll can just give these away to somebody who needs em if you don't use em—Which I doubt," Ebony hurried up and tossed that last part in there causing all of us to chuckle.

Feeling Carter pinch me to get my attention, I looked back up at him tuning Ebony and Collin out. Bashfully biting down on my bottom lip, this man still gave me tremors when I looked him in the eyes too quickly. With his left arms still slung over my shoulder, Carter palmed my belly with his right hand. Something he'd been doing since my stomach formed a tiny gut.

"You ready to go?" he asked me as I nodded my head up and down still nibbling on my bottom lip.

"Where ya'll finna go?" Collin asked us as we turned towards him.

"Home... Where yo ass should be *nigga*," Carter responded as the both of them snickered.

"Shit—I was home..." Collin smirked as he winked down at Ebony whose cheeks flashed red. "Yo ass called me—"

"You called Collin?" Ebony, and I both blurted out as Carter shrugged and smiled.

"Cuz, my Mani senses kept tingling—"

"Shut up," I nudged him as he and his brother laughed.

"Ya'll are a trip," Ebony rolled her eyes playfully as Collin flicked her nose. "*Stop*—I told you I don't like dat!" Ebony quickly formed a fist and punched Collin in his chest as he laughed.

"Dat shit ain't hurt—You weak!" He teased causing her to giggle and punch him again. "*Weak!*"

"Dis all da shit y'all got?" Carter pointed to both baskets, pulling away from me as he pulled Ebony's basket towards him.

"Yeah," I answered him as he nodded.

"Let's go... I gotta pick up Cairo," Carter ended my shopping trip instantly as I sigh left my mouth.

"*Nuh-uh*, don't do dat—"

"Do what?" I batted my eyes as I looked over at Ebony like I didn't know what she was talking about.

"Huffing like you relieved to get away from me—"

"I was not doing that!" I lied as Carter looked back at me with a smirk on his face.

"Dats what she did, Eb," Collin wasn't ever on my side unless it was going against Carter.

"No, I wasn't," I playfully rolled my eyes at Carter's brother before looking to him to defend me. "You're not gonna say anything—"

"Nope—"

"Yeah... Let's go," Carter gripped the cart with on hand and tossed the over around my waist. "Grab Ebony's, bro," Carter instructed Collin as he moved to the end of the aisle. "Tell yo sista bye and dat you'll see her next week—"

"*Shut up!*" Ebony and I both told Carter as he and Collin laughed.

"Bye Ebony," I still said it though because I had a feeling Carter probably wouldn't want me to go out until next week.

And I didn't care... I needed a break from shopping. And I wanted to eat. So as long as those things happened, today—I'd be satisfied.

"Whatchu wanna eat?" Carter asked as we walked up to the red cash registers. "Sonic?" He read my mind as I greedily licked my lips. "Fat mama—"

"Don't even!" My face was as serious as I was being but Carter still laughed at me.

"Gimme kiss—"

"No."

"You ain't miss me—"

Doesn't negate the fact that you called me fat—"

"Aw, here you go—"

"Yup, there I go."

Watching me intently, I cut my eyes up at him, and Carter did the same. Fighting the urge to smile, if I did, Carter would just lean in, peck my lips and this little stare down would be over.

"I'ma cause a scene," Carter threatened as the right side of my mouth twitched.

Keeping my lips together, I could hear the tiny voice inside of my head telling me to give in but I didn't listen.

"*I give good love... I'll buy yo baby clothes—*"

"Carter—"

"*I'll cook yo dinner too. Soon as I get home from work—I'll pay yo rent! Your faithful lover. Hoo baybeh—Soon as I get home, soon as I get home from work—*"

"OKAY!"

"*Girl I'll treat you right and I'll never lie...*" There was no stopping him. "*For all dat it's worth—*"

"I'll be in the truck," I walked off as I noticed most of the people in check-out, employees and customers watching Carter show his ass.

He was laughing and two of the older women, in line, weren't making it any better by amening his antics. Just annoying, per usual.

CHAPTER TWO

Carter

Pulling into one of Sonic's parking spaces, Amani's eyes lit up as she unbuckled her seat belt to climb over me. Laughing at her thirsty ass, I palmed her cheeks as she crawled into my lap.

"Stop," she giggled so close to my face, I snuck a kiss just to see her blush.

"How you doin' all dis when you couldn't pick yo towel up—"

"Because..." Amani twisted her lips turning her face back towards the menu to hide her smile.

"Cuz, nothin'—Yo lazy ass!" I lightly scolded, smacking her ass as she looked back at me smirking.

"Don't start nothing—"

"You ain't sayin' none butta word," I matched her freaky as she snickered, shaking her head to focus back on the menu.

Watching her side profile, my baby girl was finally puffing her mama's face out. Amani had rounder cheeks and wider nostrils. Something that you wouldn't notice if you hadn't seen her before the baby bump... Or if you didn't spend every night watching her sleep, like I did. *Shit, a nigga done turned to mush fuckin' with Shawty.*

"Do you want anything?" Amani pinched my cheek as I smirked looking out the window at the roller skating waitress waiting on me to answer Amani.

"Whatchu get?" I didn't even have to ask because I knew she ordered the All-American Dog with a large Limeade Slush. "All-American wit da Lime?" I answered my own question as Amani grinned and waggled her eyes brows causing me to smile, too.

"You do love me!" She gushed as I watched our waitress grin as she watched us interact.

"Already," I flicked Amani's chin before scooting forward so I could stick my head out the window, too. "Lemme getta... *Uh—Supersonic* double cheese witta Coke."

"Do you want tatter tots?" she asked jotting it down as I nodded. "*Okay*—You're eating here or you—"

"*To-Go!*" Amani and I both cut her off as she giggled and nodded.

"Okay—Alright... I'll have that out soon," the waitress skated away as I helped Amani back into her seat.

"Issa bout time you stop doin' dis shit," I told her as she pursed her lips together to keep from laughing. "Got my joints barkin'—"

"You better not be trying to call me fat!" Amani was paranoid about her appearance, to which my mama already hipped me to a couple months ago when her stomach started showing.

"Chill, Mani," I told her instead, remembering how sensitive she was about this subject back at target. "You look good like dat."

Hearing her smack her lips, I turned to see why she was bent out of shape, now. Being open and honest, like an open book, Mani still needed reassurance from time to time.

"What now—"

"Don't what now—I already told you *two* years!" she folded her arms over her chest as best she could because her titties was bigger and fuller now.

Licking my lips as I eyed them, I knew I wouldn't be playing too much with them tiggobiddies since they'd be full of milk. But I was hoping that after my baby girl's first birthday, Amani wouldn't go back to the itty bitty titty committee.

"My eyes," Amani lifted my chin as I goofily grinned. "Are right here."

"Dats where I was lookin'—*A'ight*," I chuckled at how serious she would jump after laughing and carrying out with me. "I'm just sayin'," I licked my lips as my eyes dropped back to her titties. "You look good enough to—"

"Here's your order!"

Flinching a little because shawty rolled over out of nowhere, Amani burst into laughter as I smacked my lips, grabbing the food from her hands.

"You're so cute together," the waitress gushed as Amani ate it up, placing her hands to her chest as she beamed with pride.

Smacking my lips and shaking my head, both women laughed. *I know we cute... Relationship goals... Allat dat shit!*

"You must not wanna tip—"

"I'll give you one!" Amani giggled as she dug into my

pocket retrieving my wallet like it was nothing. "Here," she pulled a twenty from my wallet the proceeded to crawl back onto my lap so she could hand it to the waitress whose mouth was too the floor watching the same shit I just seen. "Here," Amani jiggled the bill to get her to move towards the money. "He won't bite—Well, he won't bite you," Amani grinned seductively as she looked over her shoulder.

Nodding my head once, I couldn't deny the truth in her statement. As a matter of fact... I palmed her ass and squeezed, getting her to giggle.

"Take care," Amani told the cashier as she tried to get back to her seat.

"Nah, where you goin'?" I beckoned, not ready for my fun to end.

"Not here—"

"Then where?" My voice cracked as she laughed at me.

"Me too—But I wanna eat... Feed your baby," she pulled the baby card as I exhaled, letting go of her ass.

Snickering softly, Amani climbed back to her seat as I rolled my eyes to the side, starting up the truck and backing out. Knowing her eyes were on me, I didn't look her way. That only made her laugh even harder as I fought the urge to grin, like I wanted to. Clenching my jaw instead, I tried making this light, but I was too late. Clasping her palm to my chin, Amani squeezed then laughed when I didn't turn her way.

"In the thunder and rain..." she giggled as she sang causing me to crack a smile. *"You stare into my eyes*—Look at me!" she stopped singing to shake my face a little as I cut my eyes in her direction. "Aww, pumpkin..." Amani cooed as I smirked and shook my head.

Gazing into her eyes a slick smile spread across my face as a thought flashed in my head. Reaching up just as the light turned green, I gripped her upper thigh and squeezed getting her to screech in laughter.

"Keep singin'—*I can feel yo hand...*" I helped her out as she continued laughing. "*Movin' up my thigh—*"

"You're gonna—*Carter!*" Amani squealed because this part of her thigh was ticklish. "You're gonna make me pee—"

"Do it—"

"STOP!" She was close to tears as I let her go. "That's not even funny!" Amani hit my shoulder as I laughed at her. "I was about to pee on myself," she finished giggling while gripping her belly. "Take me home—"

"Shut up—You ain't runnin' shit... I'm takin' my baby home," I grumpily told her as she giggled and shrugged.

"Which means you gotta take *his* mama, too."

"Make me pull dis shit ova if you want to—"

"Carter!" Amani giggled as I swerved to the next lane. "Why you bein' mean to me? I just wanna eat and love you!"

"I just wanna eat and rub on yo booty—"

"It's always sexual with you!" Amani laughed with me as I nodded my head.

"Still love, though."

"*Yeah...* Tell me anything," Amani mumbled as she dug into the bag and grabbed her tatter tots.

Flicking the side of her face, she giggled and continued chomping on her food. *Good*, as long as she content, I'm good.

"Don't forget to pick up Cai," Amani reminded me as I quickly swerved out of the turning lane causing some horns to blare as I held up my hand.

"*Shit*—Fuckin' around witchu I was about to go straight home," I shook my head as Amani snorted. "Wuss allat for?"

"Because you were thinking with your little head and not your big head," she laughed at her own joke as I exhaled slowly, causing her to giggle even more. "You don't have to laugh—I know I'm funny!" Amani quickly defended self-given comedic title as I shook my head. "Shut up!"

"Lame *ah*—"

"Carter!" Amani laughed with me. "You like it."

"Yeah, I prefer a square—Y'all homebodies and I ain't gotta worry bout shit."

"Not for long," Amani shimmied in her seat, catching my glare and laughing. "Hot girl summer coming up and I'm in Texas and I'll be finer—Thicker," she ran her tongue slowly over her lips before winking over at me as I bashfully chuckled. "I might just find a lil something on the side after graduation—"

"I'ma beat yo ass when we get home," I cut her bullshitting short as she leaned to the side laughing. "Ain't shit funny, Mani—"

"Aww, babe, you know all of *this*..." Amani circled her finger around her crotch area. "Is all yours—"

"Dats why I marked my territory," I told her, palming her stomach as her face went bleak. "Shit ain't funny no more is it!" I teased as Amani groaned, rolling her eyes.

Buzzz!

SHAKING MYSELF AWAKE, Amani jolted slightly as I gripped her ankle tightly. *Shit, I ain't know I fell asleep*, I thought as I loosened the grip on her foot. Slouched to the side with part of her face tucked between her elbow, Amani's soft snores poured from her slightly opened mouth as I smirked and shook my head. Shawty was knocked out cold.

Buzzz!

I thought I heard my phone. Carefully lifting Amani's leg, I scooted to the edge of the cushion until I could set her leg down gently without waking her. Buzzing to voicemail, my phone rang twice more before I was successfully able to pick it up in the kitchen, away from Amani.

"Ma, wussup?" My face scrunched up as I caught the time on the oven.

Cairo was upstairs, probably sleeping too because the house was too quiet. Licking my lips as I made a mental note to check on him, I crossed my arms over my chest as I waited for my mama to speak. Hearing sniffles instead my antennas went up as my jaw clenched and I unfolded my arms.

"Ma?"

"I'm here..." her voice was low. "I've been—*Uh*..." She stammered as I heard her swallow. "Granny's back in hospital—"

"*Back?*" I cut in, focusing only on that word.

"*Oh...*" My mama's voice dropped an octave like I'd caught her red-handed in the cookie jar. "We didn't tell ya'll..." she exhaled as my face remained scrunched up.

"*We?* What—Ma, whatchu mean?" My right hand moved as I spoke.

She was silent but I could hear the TV going in the background so I knew she hadn't hung up. Probably trying to figure out what she was going to tell me. Nothing but the truth mattered... I didn't want to hear any excuses, especially since Granny was back in the hospital.

"Around the time David was shot, Granny slipped and fell," she explained as my mind shifted back to that time.

I remember my mama telling me about her fall and I asked was she cool. I got a nod, a smile, and a brief update but my understanding was everything was good. So my focus went back to the bullshit surrounding Yelly, Troy, and my Uncle David.

"*They* found a tumor during her CAT scan and chemo started—"

"Wait, what?" All I could focus on was the tumor. "Granny got cancer?"

My mama was silent for a second, "*Did* but she went into remission and—"

"It's back," I clenched my jaw as her silence confirmed what I'd said. "Who thought dis was a good idea to keep it from me and Collin?"

"*We* all did—"

"WHO IS WE—"

"Carter Banks, do not raise your voice at me!" My mama got louder so she could be heard. "The decision to keep *my* children from worrying about *my* mother was a collective decision by me and your father," her voice was harder. "She wasn't like she is now—"

"Whatchu mean, now?"

"Let me speak, first, and you'll know," I could tell by the squawking of her tone that she was growing impatient with me. "*Bubba*... I didn't think things would go from good to bad back to good again and quickly worsen or else I would've told you and Collin," my mama was sniffling again and calling me by my nickname so I know she was going through it.

I wasn't trying to be disrespectful or push her feelings aside... But just like she felt for her mama, that was my granny. Every memory with her was golden, and I had plenty to remember her by but I wasn't ready for them to be the only thing I had left of her. Clenching my jaw as I fought my bottom lip trying to tremble, my eyes misted until they clouded. Since birth, Granny D was my ride or die. She taught me how to drive stick, curse, and spit—And I mean revving your throat until your mucus and saliva mixed and hocking it out like boxers did in the bucket when it dinged. To be the mother to four girls, she was one of the guys. And you couldn't tell me, Collin, Chevy, or Cooper nothing because Granny D loved her boys.

"Bubba?"

"Yeah?" I sniffled, swiping the back of my hand across my eyes.

"I'm sorry..."

Nodding my head as my jaw clenched, it didn't really matter at this point. I'd miss the mark to make one last lasting memory with my granny and there were a lot of people to blame. My parents being the top two.

"It's whatever—I'ma call you later," I quickly ended the call.

Placing my phone on the island so I could palm it, I stretched my arms by bending down, keeping my hind legs shoulder length apart. Breathing in deeply, I wasn't in denial but I didn't want to believe it. Feeling a hand on my back, I shot up quickly, snapping my neck a little as I winced, startling Amani.

"Whatchu doin' up?" I asked her as she sleepily scanned my face.

"You okay?" Amani yawned as I nodded my head. "What happened to your back?"

"Nothin'—I was just... *Uh,* stretchin'," I told her as she yawned again. "C'mon—Let's go to bed—"

"It's only—Oh my *God,* we slept to ten?" Her eyes bucked as I nodded my head up and down. "Okay..." Amani shrugged like there was nothing else left to do but sleep as I smirked, slinking my arm around her waist. "You sure you okay?" she asked me as I nodded again.

"Yeah—You can't be poppin' up and shit," I told her as she calmly nodded her head as we approached the stairs. "Almost swung on you."

"I hope not," Amani grinned. "Because if it wasn't me then it'd be Cai or the baby—"

"*Tsk!*" I smacked my lips chuckling. "Da baby ain't finna tap my back dis early," I told Amani as she giggled and shrugged.

"You're gonna come to bed with me?" Amani looked up as I nodded.

"Where else I'ma go—"

"I'm just asking because you weren't by me when I woke up," she explained as I stopped the both of us to check on Cairo.

Just as I'd suspected, his ass was out cold, too. In his gaming chair with his headset still on, the controller was close to slipping out his hand as I removed it, placing it on the side table near his bed. Pulling his headset from his ears, Cairo jumped up.

"Get in da bed, boy," I chuckled as he looked around his room perplexed. "Ova there," I directed his delirious ass to his bed while laughing at him.

"Goodnight daddy—Goodnight, Mani," he said just as his face hit the pillow.

"Goodnight, baby," Amani answered him before I could. "Sleep tight, don't let the bedbugs bite."

"Goodnight, Ro—*Eh...*" I said as his head lifted but his eyes remained closed. "You cleanin' dis whole room tomorrow—Before da games and bullshit I want yo bed made, deez clothes folded and da food out," I demanded as he nodded once. "You ain't livin' in no sty and you can keep yo shit clean when you witcho mama and Grammy so I'on expect none less when you come home."

"A'ight—"

"*A'ight?*"

"*Yes, sir.*"

"A'ight, get some sleep, Ro," were the last words he heard because as soon as I stepped away from my son's bed he was snoring.

Walking out his room and closing the door, Amani was grinning from ear to ear. Walking her into our room, she never stopped smiling.

"Whatchu smilin' for?" I asked while helping her onto the bed.

"You—"

"Okay?"

"Being a daddy," she gushed while yawning, this time attempting to cover her mouth as I smirked and shrugged. "You're an amazing daddy," Amani told me like she'd done before. "I can't wait for this baby to meet you," she said as she closed her eyes. "*He's* gonna—"

"She—"

"Whatever *God* gives us," Amani tried flipping my words on me as I snorted, pulling her head onto my chest.

"Go to sleep, Mani," I breathed as she snickered then two minutes later was snoring softly.

Rubbing her back as she slept peacefully, my mind was still on my Granny and the brief phone call from my mama. Tapping my left pocket with my free hand, I used the same one to grip my right.

"*Fuck*," I whispered once I realized my phone was still on the island.

Breathing in and out, I couldn't just get up so soon after lying down so I had to wait it out. Once I was sure Amani would sleep even as the bed rocked from me getting out of it, then I'd leave. Looking to the left at the clock, I hoped it was less than twenty minutes. *Or I can just get up and act like I'm goin—*

Nestling the side of her face even more into my chest,

Amani gripped me like she could sense I was trying to leave. *Shit*! I ain't gettin' out this bed no time soon. Clenching my jaw as I continued rubbing her back, I figured this would make her comfortable enough to slip even further into her dreams. Something had to give, though.

CHAPTER THREE

Amani

Chewing on the eraser on my pencil, as I pushed my frames back. My eyes had been sliding left to right for hours, my contacts gave in. Plus the burning sensation I always felt this time of night, while I worked on my laptop didn't help, either. And I think I was out of eyedrops too. Nodding my head as I scanned over the six paragraphs I had written, I needed seven hundred more words and I didn't think I could peck another three. Opening my mouth, a yawn escaped as the palm of my hand caught the heat from the hot air I was forcing out. Eyes watering in the process, I was dead tired, but I wanted to finish this last term paper before the week was up. My baby shower was quickly approaching, and I didn't want to have any deadlines creeping up on me so suddenly.

I'd worked tirelessly for this 3.9 and I wasn't going to watch my GPA slip away from me over a day I clearly didn't need. With everything this baby already had, the baby shower, to me, was just another day for Carter's family to get together, eat, and catch up. Lowering my computer screen as I heard footsteps coming up the stairs, I could also hear low murmurs as the walking stopped completely. Lifting my chin to hear better, I cinched my eyes in confusion because I couldn't make out who Carter was on the phone with.

"Yeah, I know," I heard him say as he started walking up the steps again. "Yeah—But you'on think *she* gon' make it past then?"

Who me? My nosey self had the nerve to ask, internally.

"Nah, I'on like dem odds..." Carter sighed as he came through our bedroom door. "I mean—I know... *Damn,*" he exhaled deeply, again as my empathy antennas rose quickly.

Raising his hand to his forehead, I watched Carter use his thumb and middle finger to squeeze his temples as he breathed deeply, listening to the voice on the other end of his phone. Dropping his shoulders and hand to stare down at his right hand, I didn't like the tone of his voice. It lacked luster and I could sense he was stressed about something. Since last night, he'd been on the phone, whispering. He thought I was sleeping, and I was, partially, but I woke up a few times, to pee and heard him. He didn't even bat an eye when I used God's name in vain so I knew something bad was going on.

"A'ight, so when you goin—*Next week?*" The slight raise in his tone made me gasp, grabbing his attention as Carter's eyes locked on mine. "I'ma call you back," he quickly hung up, and I knew I was busted. "You finished yo paper?" He asked as I shook my head, nibbling on my bottom lip. "So why you listenin' so hard when you should be focusin' on yo school work?"

Dropping my jaw as I blinked twice more, I know he hadn't redirected his anger towards me. Clutching the pencil, I'd taken from my mouth, I was floored with no words to express how much Carter had me messed up.

"So you ain't got—"

"I know you're really not mad at me," I chuckled but nothing was funny.

"Who said I was mad—"

"Nobody has to say it—You're loud and rude!"

"Rude?" he skipped over addressing how loud he was, choosing to raise his voice even more as he questioned the latter. "You shouldn't be listenin' so fuckin' hard—"

"Okay, Carter, I don't care!" I yelled over him, pushing my laptop off my thigh so I could get up and go pee.

Arguing was never my steeze. You couldn't pay me to go back and forth with a person, especially if I cared about them. That little scuffle I had with Dede and her goons was out of my control but had I been privy to her antics, I'd probably took Carter's suggestion and called in that night.

"Where you goin'—"

"To the bathroom—Or are you gonna yell at me for trying to empty my freaking bladder!" I snapped my head in his direction, stopping in my tracks.

He was pushing me to the edge with his attitude and my pig-headed trait was about to rear its ugly head. I may not be confrontational but I can be stubborn as a mule. That's my toxic trait. Watching his jaw twitch I rolled my eyes and kept walking again. Barely making it to the bathroom, I plopped down on the toilet and looked up to see Carter walking in. Ignoring him, I purposely looked everywhere but him. I don't know what his problem was but I could already feel the tears burning the back of my eyeballs.

Wiping and flushing, I palmed the back of the toilet for support as I lifted myself up, causing Carter to leap forward with his arm extended. Rolling my eyes and shaking my head, I heard him huff as he moved closer to help me stand. Mad because I didn't want to be touched and because I'd never had this problem with going to the bathroom, I pushed him away.

"Whatchu doin' allat for?" Carter smacked his lips as I lathered my hands with soap, pursing my lips together.

Washing and rinsing, I could hear him breathing heavily because I wouldn't say anything. Not even look his way. And he could blame himself for the way I was acting. I was closer to my due date and graduation, and Carter chooses to do this now. I should've known better than to think the honeymoon phase would last forever. I guess that's what I get for having the baby before the wedding.

"Wait, wait—C'mere," Carter quickly grabbed ahold of me as I tried leaving the bathroom.

He knew me well enough to know I was going to fall asleep without speaking to him and probably carry this out for the rest of the week.

"I'm sorry..." he paused as I stared blankly at him. "For real—Look at me," Carter gripped my chin to stop my head turning away from him. "I'm just dealin' wit some shit—"

"So, that's what I'm here for," I cut him off as he nodded his head. "Yelling at me—"

"I ain't even yell atchu!" his voice rose to the same volume it'd been when he got off the phone as I cut my eyes up at him. "A'ight—*Damn, shit...* My fault," his apology was atrocious as my left brow rose causing him to smirk.

"I don't find any of this funny—"

"A'ight, Mani..." Carter breathed deeply, as I waited for

him to get himself together long enough to apologize to me. "I'm sorry... For real, Shawty," Carter pulled me into him so that his breath tickled the skin on my face when he spoke. "I just been dealin' wit dis shit..." he stopped talking, and I hoped he would continue.

I'd gone through being shut out before with Brandon and although Carter has shared things with me, I'm sure he's never told anybody else... I didn't want him to think he couldn't come to me when things got tough for him. Especially when he hadn't gotten over the trying times.

"Tell me..." I urged him as I watched his chest cave and his bottom lip to tremble. "Carter—*Babe!*" I gasped noticing the glossiness in his eyes as he let me go to cover his face. "Carter!" I tried pulling on his arm to get his hand to fall but I couldn't.

Floored, I didn't know what to do at this point. *Was he really crying?* Listening to his muffled sniffles, I had no choice but to confirm my assumption. What the hell? I've never witnessed a man crying in front of me—Ever! My heart leaped from my chest as I got closer to him, hooking my hands to his arms and gently yanking. To my surprise, this worked. Carter's face was beet red—Eyes swollen and sulking, I was crushed. Swallowing my own tears back, my bottom lip started to tremble too.

"Whatchu bout to cry for?" Carter poked my cheek laughing as two tears fell from my eyes before I snorted laughing.

"I don't know?" my voice was shrill as my shoulders rose. "You're crying so... I don't know," I told him again, as he used his thumb to swipe my tears away. "I'm not gonna leave you," I assured him just in case this was the reason behind his tears.

Staring blankly back at me, Carter's head went back as he croaked, causing more tears to fall from his eyes as I wondered what place the weeping was coming from. Was it still sorrow or was he amused?

"I know you not..." he told me as he pulled the front of his shirt up to wipe his face. "But it's nice to know—"

"Carter, shut up!" I groaned as he grinned, still wiping his face. "What's wrong?"

Quietly lifting his shoulders, I exhaled deeply, seeing most of his teeth as he smiled back at me. I hated when he did that because I didn't know what mood he was in. Just wondering raised my anxiety a little more than usual.

"My mama called me last night..." Carter paused to wet his lips with his tongue. "My granny back in da hospital—"

"Are you serious?" I don't know why I gasped, but it just seemed appropriate.

"Yeah... She not gon' make it back home either," his head dropped as he told me that and I could see his face twitching as he fought the urge to drop more tears.

Reaching up and cupping his face, I didn't know what to tell him but I was willing to do whatever it took to make him feel better. Rubbing his cheek with my thumb, Carter reached up, placing his hand on top of mine as he gripped it, lowering my palm to his lips so he could kiss it. Biting my bottom lip, I couldn't stop my eyes from smiling.

"Where does she live?"

"Houston—"

"Let's go there!" I jumped to the best suggestion in my book.

"Nah, shawty," Carter immediately smacked his lips, rejecting my suggestion as my shoulders fell disappointedly.

"Why not?" I needed a solid answer, otherwise I'd keep pushing for this.

"Cuz—Whatchu mean?" Carter dropped my hand as he took a step back to point at my belly.

"Okay, I'm pregnant... *And?*"

"*And*... We like six weeks away from delivery—"

"Houston is in Texas!" I shouted over him, hating that he was dead set on treating me like our home was a hospice and I didn't have any other choice but to be here.

I had to give up going to class for online classes. I couldn't stray too far from him without him popping up, regardless of who I was with. And most of the time it was his brother's girlfriend or his mother. Still, Carter had to see with his own eyes if I was doing just fine and even then, he'd still find a way to put a limit or boundaries on whatever I wanted to do while I was carrying his child. And I'll admit, this is partially my fault because I do love him and most of the time, I wanted to be around him... But right now, my main focus was on him getting his last goodbye from his Granny because I'll be doggone if he went through the five stages of grief and held anything over my head.

"How far is Houston from—"

"Mani, just drop it—"

"NO!" I grabbed his arm because now he was the one trying to get out of the bathroom. "You didn't just cry for nothing, Carter..." my voice was calmer but there was a sense of urgency in my tone I desperately needed for him to pick up on. "You need to see her—I'll be fine," I assured him as he shook his head. "If you don't then I'll never forgive you."

"How you gon' do dat and you'on even know Granny," Carter chuckled as I shrugged.

"*See*, right there." I caught him before he said another thing. "Perfect reason to always hold this over your head," I snapped my finger as he'd given me the best excuse to always use against him when I wanted to be mad for no reason. "You're crying over her so I know she was amazing and if you don't give me the chance to meet her before—"

"A'ight, a'ight, a'ight..." Carter's hand rose to shut me up as I pursed my lips together sternly.

Exhaling as he ran his fingers through his hair, I know he'd worry about me but this mattered more. I'd be fine. I know that much. I didn't gain but thirty pounds and although I felt fat on most days, I could still fit into most of my prenatal clothes.

"We're doing this whether you want to or not," I told him as I released his arm to waddle out the bathroom.

"Who you talkin' to?" Carter was on my heels, poking my sides where I was most ticklish as I giggled, swatting at his fingers before making it to the bed.

"Who else—"

"You real bold—Whatchu say... *Freaking bladder!*" Carter was back to his regularly annoying self as I rolled my eyes to the side to keep from laughing. "*Hoo... Guess you told me, huh?*"

"Shut up," I giggled as Carter pulled me into a hug.

Pecking the tip of my nose, he dipped his head down again, swallowing it whole as I scrunched up my face, smiling as he pulled back.

"I love you."

Since the first time he spoke those three words to me, Carter always beat me to say them. And I always had to piggyback with...

"I love you, too."

"Now get up there so I can blow dat back out!" Carter twirled me towards the bed as I giggled loudly.

"Stop."

"Nah," he shook his head while pushing me on the bed. "Dis da test to see if you can handle three—Shit, almost four hours in da truck," he told me as he loosened the drawstrings to his sweats.

"We're not doing this for four hours—"

"You gon' do what I tell you to do," Carter barked over me

as he crawled on top of me, nipping at the skin on my neck and face as I laughed. "Take all dis shit off!" He plucked my shirt as I pushed myself back to sit up. "Lay back down—"
"Okay, so how will I take my clothes off?"
"Dats five—"
"What?"
"Every time you talk back I'm addin' an hour—"
"That's ridiculous—"
"*Six—*"
"Carter—"
"*Seven!*"
"Stop it—"
"*Eight!*"

Cutting my eyes up at him as Carter hovered over me smiling, I was not about to play these games with him. *I'm just glad he's in a better mood, though.*

"Eight and a half," Carter told me as I giggled. "You talkin' shit in yo head so I'ma—"

"No, I'm not!" I protested as his lips touched mine. "Be careful," I poked his nose as he lifted some of his weight off me. "I love you—"

"Nah, don't even try it!" Carter chuckled as I giggled. "Turn around."

CHAPTER FOUR

Carter

Helping Amani out the car, Cairo was right behind me, grabbing her other hand. She giggled as me walked her to the door, too. I know she probably thought I viewed her as hopeless but that wasn't the case. Amani just moved too slow for me, now and if I didn't have her hand, leading us around, she'd be waddling behind me, out of breath ready to kill me. Approaching the triage desk, the nurse waiting already had a welcoming smile on her face.

"Well, hello!" she gushed eyeing Amani's big belly. "Are we ready for delivery?" She asked as Amani's face fell flat causing me to laugh.

"Four more weeks," Amani's tone was low as I continued smiling to egg her on.

"*Oh—I'm so sorry!*" the nurse quickly apologized but she couldn't remove the sting Amani felt nor take away the humor she'd caused me.

"I'm just here to see my granny," I told the nurse as she jolted her mouse to wake the screen.

"What's her name?"

"Dorothy Jean Kramer—"

"*Grandma Dot* is your grandmother?" The nurse cheesed as I nodded my head with a smile. "*Oh*, we just love her here!" she told me while picking up her phone to dial four buttons. "How are ya, this mornin'—Yeah? Really..." The nurse's face dropped as she looked up at the three of us. "Do you feel up to visitors—*What's your name?*" she asked me while covering the receiver part of the phone.

"*Bubba*," I told her as Cairo snickered and Amani giggled just because my son's laughter was contagious.

"It's *Bubba—*"

"*Bubba's here!*" I smiled as Granny's voice picked up over the phone.

"I'll send him up!" the nurse giggled, now holding the phone up with her shoulder so she could write on her notepad. "Here," she handed me the slip. "Use the elevators to the left. Third floor."

"Thank you—"

"No, problem!"

"You ready?" I asked Amani's whose face was showing just how nervous she was.

"Yeah," Cairo answered knowing I wasn't talking to him but we laughed, anyway.

"Shut up," I told him as Amani's face relaxed a little more.

Ding!

The elevator door opened as Cairo and I allowed Amani to walk off first. Nodding for Ro to get out before me, I rejoined them taking Amani's right side as I grabbed her hand with my left and led the way into Granny's room. Already sitting up with a smile on her face, it was hard not to mirror her expression but I couldn't help but notice her deteriorating frame. Bald and frail, this wasn't my Granny. Blinking back tears as she stretched her arms out to me, if I cried it'll only mean I accepted her fate and I wasn't ready to do that, just yet. Today was about her meet—

"Who's this?" Granny pointed at Amani who shyly looked over at me. "Your mama ain't tell me you was havin' another one!" Granny coughed as I embraced her. "You can squeeze me, *Bubba* I ain't snapped in two, yet!" she held me tighter as I chuckled and squeezed a little more than I had before. "Hold on," she told me as we stayed in this position. "I got a full year of hugs I need to get out," she told me and I couldn't hold my tears back. "Aw, don't you dare—Hush now..." Granny rubbed the top of my head as I held her close to my heart. "I'm still here —Look at me," Granny pushed me upward as her hands went from my head to my cheeks. "I know y'all had a helluva year and I'm not holdin' no grudges, *Bubba—I can't,*" she chuckled and coughed, using the inside of her shirt to cover her mouth. "I'm goin' home to glory but I'm here for the time bein' cuz I knew my *Big Bubba Baby* needed one last time—"

"Don't say last," I cut her off as Granny quickly pursed her lips together seriously.

"You're really gonna be a cry baby in front of your baby— Babies?" Granny put me on the spot as I turned around to see Cairo and Amani tearing up.

"They cryin' too," I shrugged as Granny and I laughed.

"Who's that?" she whispered to me as my smile grew wider. "Ahhh—Why wasn't I invited to the wedding?" Granny pinched my cheek and shook it.

Wincing at the slight pain she was causing, I had to laugh because Granny hadn't changed mentally. Physically, yeah, but she was still crazy and I loved every second of it.

"*Ah—Sss, ouch!*" I cracked up laughing with Granny as she stopped shaking my face and removed her fingers from my cheeks. "We ain't married—"

"You still bringin' babies into this world out of wedlock!" Granny scolded as my head hung low. "Carter, I thought I schooled you better than that," she flicked my chin as I nodded my head. "Eighteen, I get it—But you're touching thirty."

"*Tsk!* In four years," I blew out air as Amani giggled. "You be quiet—"

"No, you hush—Step up here, baby," Granny motioned for Amani to walk up. "Cairo, you come hug me, too—You know who I am!" she told my son as he smirked and ran up to the side of the bed where me and Mani stood.

Wrapping his small, skinny arms around Granny, she kissed the top of his head and rubbed his hair like she'd done to me, first. Smiling as I watched them, I looked towards Amani, reaching for her hand to hold. She was right. I did need this— We all needed this. And I probably would displace my anger had we not drove down here and Granny passed away without me getting this chance to talk to her.

"*I love you,*" I mouthed to her as she flushed red, bowing her head once and winking up at me.

"What ya'll doin'—Talkin' shit about me?" Granny was watching me and Amani interact as I laughed and shook my head. "What? Ya'll don't like my hair?" Granny slowly turned her head around as Cairo squealed in laughter because she didn't have any hair.

"Granny, chill," I chuckled as I squeezed Amani's hand. "Dis is, Mani—"

"Mani?" Granny spoke her name as Amani nodded her head. "Where ya from, baby?"

"Chicago—"

"Chi-town's finest!" Granny was funnier than me. "I've been up there a few times—"

"Doin' what?" I cut in as Granny batted her eyes before rolling them.

"Don't worry ya self with my business," Granny sassed as I smirked and nodded.

"You was bein' fast—"

"That I was but it resulted in some beautiful times—"

"*Ugh!* I'on wanna hear dat," I groaned as Granny and Amani giggled.

"Same as what you two are doin'—Or were doin'… When's *she* comin'?" Granny palmed Amani's belly as I grinned looking down at her. "What?" Granny asked after she noticed the glare Amani was giving me.

"They keep arguin' ova what da baby gon' be," Cairo, still leaning into Granny's bed as she rubbed his head with her left and palmed Amani's belly with her right, explained to her.

"Oh, so y'all didn't officially find out?"

"No, but it's definitely a boy," Amani nodded with Cairo as I shook my head, looking over at Granny.

"How ya know?" Granny asked Mani who shrugged. "So, you can't be that sure—"

"Sure enough—I mean, Carter is the same only he's team girl," Amani told my Granny who giggled and shrugged.

"She said *sure enough*," Granny turned towards me as I smiled. "I don't mind, either way," Granny told Amani whose face had gone from shy to grinning. "So, why you all the way out here?"

Inhaling, Amani's shoulders rose then fell as she licked her lips after exhaling.

"I used to wonder that myself but... I don't know if Chicago is my home anymore. Carter sold me a dream, and I bought it," Amani told my Granny as my face scrunched up. "Why are you looking like that?"

"What dream I sold you, Shawty?" I asked her as her shoulders dropped.

"The reality we're currently living," Amani winked and I couldn't stop myself from blushing as Granny laughed.

Wearing a silly grin to mask my embarrassing moment, I couldn't tone down the color in my cheeks. Wetting my lips as Amani reached up to pinch my cheeks, she wasn't making this shit any easier.

"So when's the wedding?" Granny blurted out as Amani's eyes bucked. "You know I can't afford to wait too much longer—"

"Granny stop," I hated hearing her talk like this.

"Well, I'm just—" Granny's coughing brought her words to life as I clenched my jaw, feeling Amani squeezing my hand, to calm me down.

Gazing down into her eyes, Granny's words truly started resonating with me. There was no way I could get her up to Dallas and back without adding to the stress her health was already under. Looking away from Amani as my mind sifted through several thoughts, I thought back to the day Troy came to my crib with his papers. He got me to thinking about my own situation with Amani and how I'd been telling her she was going to be mine forever.

"Hold up, right quick," I told Amani and Granny as I pulled Cairo along with me. "We'll be right back."

"Where we goin'?" Cairo couldn't wait to ask as we jogged to the elevator.

"To da truck," I told him just as the doors opened for us.

"Why?"

"You'll see once we get there," I told him tapping my foot impatiently as the ride down took longer than the ride up.

Clenching my jaw and checking the time on my phone, this hoe was taking way too long. Inhaling, the door dinged but we were cut off by a stampede of doctors and nurses trying to get in.

"Damn, hol'up!" I tried pushing through with my son before they got on to no avail. "Wait!" I called out just as the door was closing.

Punching the open button the doors slid back, and Cairo and I were able to get off. Fixing my clothes, my son did the same as I smirked and shook my head. Calmly swaggering off, Cairo was right beside me, out the hospital and over to the truck. I popped the locks, heading to the passenger's side where the glove box was located. Pulling it down, I rifled through some miscellaneous items like napkins, sauce packets, and bills I didn't open because I paid all my shit online…

"Here it is!" I gleefully grabbed the manilla folder I was looking for. "Hold dis," I told Cairo as I continued digging, pulling most of everything out until my hands touched velvet. "Already!" I cheered, lazily stuffing the shit I'd taken out back into the glove box before closing it. "Let's go!" I told Cairo while grabbing the folder from his hands.

Running, this time, Cairo and I both were doubling over with our palms to our knees, inside the elevator trying to catch our breaths. Taking deep breaths, I wasn't out of shape but it's been a minute since I just ran. Cairo should have my experience in this field since this lil nigga still had recess and basketball practice.

"A'ight, so look…" I tapped his shoulder to get his attention as I stood up straight. "When we get up there, I wantchu to have dis inside ya pocket," I took the velvet box from mine and handed it over to him. "Don't open it—Just hold onto it," I quickly told my nosey son as he grinned up at me and nodded.

"Wuss dis a ring?" He asked as I curled the left side of my mouth while cutting my eyes as Cairo giggled.

"You bout to find out," I told him as he grinned even harder.

DING!

"Let's go," I nodded for Cairo to walk off first as I lingered close behind him, scanning the desk outside Granny's room. "Go inside," I told Cairo as he turned over his shoulder to look for me.

Waiting for him to go in, I stopped in front of the desk, waiting for one of the three nurses to see me. The brown skin one turned quickly with a slick grin on her face. Returning the gesture, I didn't keep it too long so she wouldn't get the wrong idea.

"How y'all doin'?" I now had all of their attention.

"We fine, now," brown skin licked her lips as I chuckled softly, shaking my head.

"First, I need a pen—Thank you."

"No problem," she was still flirting, and I tried not to slip into the same trap because I couldn't be the same way without even thinking about it.

Amani was always sure to throw a fit and blow up about it later on in the day when I did flirt. And that shit was like breathing for me. A smile here and wink there—Biting my lip and shit. It's how I got her.

"Is there a priest or clergyman available?"

"You want the last rites read to Grandma Dot?" the blonde closer to the computer asked as I shrugged.

"Not quite but close—Can he stop by Granny room, like now?" I wonder as she nodded, picking up the phone.

"Sure... I'll page him up."

"A'ight cool—Thanks," My bottom lip slipped in my mouth as Brown skin played with her hair, twirling the curls around her finger.

"You're welcome..." she paused to hear my name, but I knew that game and chose to back away, instead.

She was easy on the eyes but not worth throwing away what I had at home. Beauty, brains, and brawn. The big three. And that's all a nigga needed. Hiding the manilla folder behind my back as I sauntered into the room, Granny and Amani were laughing, having a good ole time.

"If it isn't the man of the hour!" Granny spotted me first as I looked over at Cairo, hoping this nigga didn't come in here to reveal the ring I told him to keep in his pocket.

"Where were you—"

"Whatcha got behind your back?" Granny cut Amani off as her eyes dropped to the spot where I was hiding the folder.

"Just somethin' you put back on my mind."

"Is that right?" Granny sat up a little more and Amani helped fluff her pillow as she smiled over at me nodding as if to tell me, *she's the one.*

Best believe, I already knew that. That's why I was about to get this proposal and marriage out of the way so we could focus on bringing our baby girl into the world. Pulling the manilla folder out, I used the movable table and set it down. Opening the pen, my eyes scanned over the legal jargon the clerk's office explained to me on the day I paid for the certificates. I only cared for the spots I needed to sign and initial.

"Here," I held the pen out to Amani as she twisted her lips, tiptoeing over to where I was standing.

It took her three seconds to realize what I'd signed as she gasped, taking two steps back with her hands cover her mouth.

"C'mon," I urged as she laughed into her hands while shaking her head. "Why not—"

"You're not serious!" She breathed slowly as I nodded my head, careful not to laugh because she'd think this was a joke. "No," she shook her head as I nodded again. "Carter, stop—"

"What am I doin'?"

"For real?" I could see her eyes glistening and knew the tears would follow. "Carter—"

"Mani, c'mon, Shawty, I been tellin' you what it was."

Pushing the table over to her, Granny could now look over her bed at the papers to see what was driving Amani up the wall. Smiling bigger than me, Granny gently pushed Amani over towards the table as she turned back to look at her.

"Go ahead," she winked as Amani finally broke and started crying.

"*But*—Are you..." her shoulders dropped as she took the pen from my hand. "*We*..."

I felt like I could see Amani's heart leaping out of her chest as she stared down at the documents. I didn't have any doubt in my mind that she wanted too but I could allow her a couple more minutes of shock. I did spring it on her with no warning.

"Once I sign it, then what?" she asked me.

"I'ma mail it off and a week from today you gon' have my last name—"

"*A week?*" Granny and Amani repeated as I nodded my head.

"It takes longer—"

"I gotta guy," I cut Granny off as she snorted and shrugged.

"Is this legal—"

"You askin' too many questions, Mani—You gon' be my

wife or break my heart?" I dropped my eyes to the floor for dramatic effects as she giggled.

"I knew this was a ring!" Cairo blurted out, getting everybody's attention.

"*Wait*, he was in on this too?" Amani pointed towards Cairo as I shook my head.

"He just holdin' da ring—Dat I told him to keep in his pocket," I eyed Cairo as he twisted his lips looking away from me. "Fucked up my whole plan," I smacked my lips as Granny giggled and pointed over at Cairo who was trying not to laugh. "Give it here," I demanded as he quickly skipped towards me with the box in hand. "Get outta here," I flicked the back of his head as he laughed, running back to Granny as she held her arms open to receive him. "You signed dem papers?" I turned towards Amani who was dropping the pen and nodding her head. "C'mere," I extended my arms out and waited for Amani to walk into them.

Holding her tightly, she sniffled against my chest, and I knew she was crying. I wanted to, but I didn't. I'd cried enough. Hearing this one particular song inside my head, I would usually sing but I wanted her to hear and feel what I felt when I heard this song.

"Hold up," I held my finger up in the air, pulling away from Amani to dig into my pocket. "I ain't gon' sing but I gotta song for you," I told her as I scrolled through my playlists.

Hearing Granny snickering, I glanced over at her and caught a wink and blushed. *Here it is!* I exclaimed internally when I found the song I was looking for. The soft strumming of an acoustic guitar filled the semi-silent hospital room, drowning out the heart monitor and beeping and hissing of all the other machines Granny was hooked up to.

> *Embedded in my brain, I told myself I was*
> *through loving you*
> *Found myself crawling right back to you, yeah*
> *You hurt me so good, that's why I can't leave you*
> *You got me so weak like I need you*
> *Maybe I'm addicted to the pain, oh, oh, oh*

Watching the look on Amani's face go from happiness to confusion, I pulled her into my arms, anyway. Humming along with the song, I could sense Amani wasn't really feeling the first verse, and she showed me when she lifted her head up to look at me. Still perplexed, I smacked my lips because I didn't want her to ruin this moment with her overthinking.

"Why you lookin' like dat?" I asked, lining my pelvis with her belly, so we could sway from side to side.

"When have I ever hurt you?" Amani was in her head too deep to live in the moment.

Dropping my head to laugh, I knew this girl too well to think she'd be cool with the words.

"Don't laugh—I'm serious."

"I know... But you had yo moments—"

"Name one!" Amani challenged, giving me a scowl to let me know she wasn't in the mood.

Nodding my head as our eyes met, "You'on think it hurt to see you feenin' for dat nigga, BJ when you had me standin', out in da cold—" I added for comedic effects, getting Amani to laugh. "Ready to love you—"

"*Oh*, my gosh..." Amani exhaled, rolling her eyes towards the tiled ceiling. "Here we go—"

"Yeah, *here we go*," I mimicked her while flicking her chin to get her to look back at me. "Then you kept da best shit dat happened to you from me—And come to find out... BJ was witchu when yo pops pulled up!" I reminded myself of just how foul Amani was moving when we first started out.

She was playing me like a square. Like I was BJ and I ain't never cared to name niggas or pick at ex's but me and that muhfucka was apples and oranges. You knew the difference immediately. Thoroughbred, that's how I my daddy brought me up. I wasn't put on to this shit I was born into. A man of my word, even while laughing, I meant everything I said. Quote me if you will but know I will never back down or backtrack. Talk circles or renege. That's Carter Solomon Banks, born September 29th, 1994 to Solomon and Megan Banks. The realest nigga next to my blood brother and cousins... All Banks. That's on Dem Boyz—Dem Bankroll Boyz.

"To be fair, that was completely out of my control," Amani pinched my cheeks, pulling me out of my head as my face softened and I chuckled a little.

"Cut dat out—Don't be hittin' me cuz I'm right."

"You're not right—That wasn't intentional," Amani told me as my jaw twitched and I nodded my head. "It wasn't—"

"A'ight."

"But signing my name and taking your name, is... And that's what I want you to focus on from this day forward," Amani told me as I shrugged causing her to laugh. "Don't do that—"

"Nah, don't try to change da subject—"

"I'm not!" she giggled with me. "I'm sorry if I ever made you feel any kind of way—That was never my intent, Carter. Like, I really, really liked you after you threw me out of the hotel room and—"

"Bent you ova da bar—"

"Stop," Amani's teeth and lips cinched together as she looked over her shoulder to see Granny and Cairo tuning in.

"That's not even funny," she pinched me again as I laughed even more.

A'ight, a'ight," I chuckled one last time before getting serious, enough.

"And even with *you know who* popping up at my job," Amani spoke in code as best she could as I caught my son's eyes. "I knew there was no getting rid of you—"

"You tried to get rid of me?"

"No—"

"Well word dat shit differently," I told Amani as she giggled, shaking her head.

"Okay, how about…" she hummed, tucking her bottom lip into her mouth. "I knew I loved you more than ever…"

"Dats better," I leaned into her face, pecking her nose as she giggled softly.

> *I just want you to know that*
> *Everything's about you, baby*
> *Everything's about you*
> *Everything's about you…*

I mouthed the lyrics to Amani as her eyes sparkled with unshed tears. The joy I felt was insurmountable. This woman made everything better. Simple shit I didn't usually do, I wanted to just because Mani was there for me to do them for. I usually slept at my parents but with Amani here, I felt like a real grown ass man. I had a family to come home to and not just my son, at my mama and daddy's house. Shit was looking real familiar like I was finally beginning to live up to my father's name.

Knock. Knock.

Looking over at the door, together, the flirty nurse poked her head through the door, smiling before she noticed Amani in my arms. Face cracked, her mouth moved a few times before she closed it, blinking. Despite the envy you could see in her eyes, the love in the room was radiating. You could see it, feel it—Even smell its sweet aroma.

"The clergyman is here—"

"Oh, yeah," I pulled back, halfway, keeping my left hand at the small of my back. "Send him in," I urged the nurse as she nodded quickly, opening the door wider. "I got da papers," I pointed towards the bedside table near Granny who hadn't stopped smiling since we came into her room. "Granny you gon' be my witness, right?" My head tilted towards her as she giggled and nodded.

"The best there is!" she sprung up, slowly, as I moved her way to ease her lifting by pulling the pillow behind her up. "Gimme dat pen!"

"Here you go," I handed it to Granny as her shaking hand took it from my hands.

"Thank you, *Bubba*," she kissed my cheek before she started signing.

"I can't have my favorite girl missing out on one of da best days of my life," I winked, causing her to blush and knuckle my cheek for bringing her to blush as I laughed. "I love you—"

"Who doesn't!" Granny made me laugh.

And I couldn't deny her words. There wasn't a person I could call today who didn't love Granny D. Dot Kramer was an OG, respected by many and loved by all. That's how I'll always remember her and that's how Amani will know her.

CHAPTER FIVE

Amani

Pecking on the keys to my laptop, my eyes kept falling from the screen to my left ring finger. The gleaming, rose-colored, heart-cut diamond sitting inside a size-six diamond encrusted band had all my attention. *I'm a married woman!* Is all I kept thinking. MARRIED! M-A-R-R-I-E-D! The levels of shock I was feeling were beyond even being Carter's girlfriend... And it had taken me months of getting used to saying that—Let alone, the joys of finding somebody remotely close to my husband. *Husband... Such a silly word to say.*

"Whatchu smilin' for?" Carter walked in on my private thoughts as I looked up to see him grinning.

Shuffling over to the bed, he climbed in as I sat my laptop to the side, cheesing extra hard. Lying his head in my lap, I rubbed the side of his face as he did his favorite thing... Cradling my stomach, kissing near the navel and holding his private conversations, he purposely spoke loud enough for me to be privy to them too. Running my fingers through his hair, I usually spent their time together wondering who the baby would take after. My guess was Carter, since Cairo was his doppelgänger... But I couldn't think past the ring on my finger. Combing through his slick, ebony hair, the pink seemed brighter.

"*Oww*," I rubbed my left leg over the right as Carter snickered. "Stop pinching me!" I giggled as he sat up, resting his back to the headboard like me.

"I had to getcho attention," he told me as I rolled my eyes, causing him to smirk even more. "Whatchu so lost in space about?"

Lifting my shoulders, I knew why but I couldn't put it into words, just yet. I'd often found myself crying from how happy this man has made me but last Tuesday. In the midst of one of his darkest hours, he somehow made a way to make it all about me. And I would always be content with being in his presence, if that's all I got, for the rest of our time on this earth together... But Carter never failed at showing me just how much I meant to him. He'd rearranged his whole life to put me in it, giving me space to breathe and offering whatever help he could when I needed it. No matter how much he playfully annoyed me and even when he actually got on my nerves... None of that was enough to want to leave him. And I've probably told myself this a million times but Carter was the man I wanted to spend the rest of my life with. Give him all the babies he couldn't stop asking me for and just stay tucked in our own little world with visits from his mama and daddy and brother and Ebony. And my sisters too...

"You talked to Julian?" Carter pulled me from my thoughts as I took my glasses off.

"My daddy?" I asked him as he shook his head, and my face screwed in confusion. "Who then?"

"*Julián Muñoz—*"

"Stop playing!" I giggled as he snorted. "That's my daddy—"

"No, I'm yo daddy!" Carter talked over me as we laughed even more. "Dat muhfucka just came in da picture."

Twisting my lips up at him, I knew he was joking but there was a twinge of real he wanted me to pick up on. Not that Carter disliked my father because he didn't, but he always told me to guard my heart whenever I spoke with him. And at first, I thought he was being territorial and jealous but after I ran out of the dinner, Julian called four days after to ask me what was wrong. When I told him what Jomari told me, he made multiple excuses for her. One being that she needed to adjust to me coming into the family so suddenly. Then he suggested that we meet outside of everyone and gradually graft me in. *One*, I wasn't just plopped into his life—According to his mother and sisters, they'd known me, held me and even witnessed my birth. *Two*, I wasn't a secret... So before he even came looking for me, he should've put everything into perspective—Including his bratty daughter. And three, I just didn't feel like going through the motions with anybody else.

"He texted me—"

"And said?" Carter wasn't going to let me drop this subject.

"He just sent me e-gift cards and told me he'd come if he could—"

"More excuses," Carter shook his head as I exhaled softly. "Don't be sighin' and shit—"

"Because it's not that big of a deal," I scoffed, knowing I was a little hurt by hearing my father wouldn't be coming to my baby shower. "If I was in Chicago—"

"Nah..." Carter shook his head as I stopped talking. "Don't even do dat—He ain't comin' because he ain't comin'... Dis ain't got shit to do witchu livin' down here."

Pursing my lips together as my eyes dropped, I could see the gleaming ring on my finger and no longer wanted to talk about my daddy. I didn't dislike him because he wasn't coming, he probably really couldn't make it. But at least he made an effort and sent me gift cards. Two-hundred dollar gift cards each, at that. Whether I'm being too gullible or not, I'm not even there to deal with it. I'm here, with Carter... And if I'm not quick on my feet, he's always here to catch me when I fall.

"I still think—"

"That you're putting too much thought into it and that we should talk about this ring on my finger and how I made all your dreams come true!" I interjected as Carter chuckled.

"How you make all my dreams come true?"

"By becoming your wife!" I squealed, jumping into his lap, forgetting that I was eight months pregnant.

"Damn—*Mani!*" Carter scolded through laughter as I held my stomach after he almost kneed it. "You better calm down!" he pointed into my face as I giggled while holding my head down. "Shit, bout to squish my baby and shit!"

Lifting my eyes, I nibbled on my bottom lip in hopes that my sad face would shift his mood. Fighting with the corners of my mouth, I couldn't stare into his eyes this long without— *Dang it!* A huge smile spread across my face as I covered it with my hand.

"Quit playin'," Carter's shoulders dropped as he gazed into my eyes.

He's been doing this since we left Houston and I knew his

mind was stuck on Granny D. After the laughs we shared last week, I felt a twinge of his sadness too. She was truly an amazing person, and I hated that we wouldn't get to know each other past a hospital room.

Feeling Carter peck my lips, I got out of my head to see why. Sitting cowgirl style, Carter's arms were wrapped around my waist to keep us close.

"Thank you," he told me as I nodded my head.

"For what?"

"You were right."

"As always—"

"Say, Shawty… Don't get big headed," Carter laughed with me. "But, I needed to see Granny," his jaw clenched as he fought with the rest of his words. "And even though I hate sayin' dis shit but I know that's prolly da last time I'd laugh wit her," his eyes dropped as I instinctively leaned into him, kissing him back.

Cupping his cheeks in my palms, Carter looked back up at me as I gave him a reassuring smile. Grief is never easy, I know from experience. And I bet, if Jewel was a more loving mother, her death wouldn't have been as easy to put in the back of my mind. There were times when I cried but I attributed most of those sad tears to my hormones and pregnancy. Before the baby, I'd get sad at random times but I didn't cry for my mother like some people may have thought. Our relationship was complicated and most times I found myself asking why she didn't do this or that or just didn't raise my sisters and I normally. Frustrated is a better word to use than sad. Especially with my daddy being thrown into the mix. Even as a grown woman, you never stop needing a mother in your life. Somebody who's been through most of the things you believe only you're going through. I have Carter's mom and she's a gem but still… *I'll be that for my daughter when I have one.*

"Whatchu thinkin' about?" Carter was doing that thing where he watched my face for any change in emotion.

"Just mommy things," I exhaled figuring there was no use in hiding it from him.

"Like?" He pulled me closer to nestle his nose into the crook of my neck.

"I don't know..." I sighed as he pulled back to show me the frown on his face. "I mean... I don't, Carter," I bit down on my bottom lip.

"Whatchu don't know? *Huh?* You havin' second thoughts?" Carter slipped his hands underneath my shirt pressing his cold hand to my back as I flinched. "Sorry," he apologized with laughter in his tone. "Lemme warm my hands up—"

"No," I giggled trying to move in a way that he'd get off me but he wouldn't. "Why are you always cold?"

"Cuz I'ma cool ass nigga," he started cockily as I rolled my eyes. "But fuck allat—Wuss on ya mind?"

"What if I have the baby and I don't love him as much as I should?" I could feel my bottom lip quivering as Carter's hard face softened. "Like you know... I see girls with postpartum do unspeakable—"

"Dassit right there," Carter cut me off as I scrunched up my face in confusion.

"What?"

"*Unspeakable*... So you shouldn't speak those things into existence," he was giving me this biblical jargon, and I didn't need to hear that. "Nah, don't do dat—Mani, no matter whatchu feel... I'm not leavin' you witta baby," he told me while taking one of his hands out of my shirt to wipe my tears away. "So, whenever, if ever—You feel like dis shit is too much... I'ma be right here and my mama and my daddy and Ebony and Collin," he shrugged it off like it was nothing as I smirked, trying to picture his brother handling a baby. "Wuss so funny?"

"I'm just trying to picture Collin with the baby," I giggled as Carter smirked.

"Believe it or not but bro good wit da babies—Ro used to be his lil roll dawg," Carter told me as my eyes lit up. "Boffum used to ride around da city together," he laughed just thinking about it. "You gon' be straight—And I won't put too much on you dat you can't handle... Even when I be jokin' witchu," Carter was being serious now. "You want two years in between..." he nodded his head, "I'll give you eighteen months—"

"Shut up!" I giggled with him. "I knew you weren't going to give me the full two!" I pinched his side as he jerked a little, still laughing.

"Issa compromise, Shawty... I ain't finna be pullin' out every damn time," he told me as he rolled his hips. "Can't keep wastin' da seed or else God ain't gon' be happy wit me—"

"And you really shouldn't pick and choose which verses you live by," I added as I cut my eyes at him.

"Which ones I'm neglectin' since you know so much?" Carter asked as he poked my side to make me laugh.

"Babies out of wedlock—premarital sex, also known as fornication... The list goes on," I shrugged like I'd made the best points of my life as Carter's face fell flat and underwhelmed causing me to giggle.

"*Baby girl* ain't here, yet, talkin' bout *da list goes on*—And did you forget?" Carter lifted my left hand with the hand he used to wipe my tears. "*Yous married now.* And I expect you to carry ya self as a married woman—Meanin' all official documents changed, ya license shouldn't read *Rahim*."

"I was going—"

"*I was gonna* nonthin'—Das an excuse," Carter cut me off as I giggled. "I bet yo school name still listed under Rahim, too—"

"Yeah because we just got our license back! I can't tell them something I don't have documented proof of!"

"But you keep smilin' at dat ring, claimin' you happy to make my dreams comes true—"

"Shut up!" I doubled over laughing with him. "You know I'm ecstatic!" I winked at him as he smacked his lips before muffing me. "Whatever, you know the truth—"

"No, what I know is dem documents—"

"Okay, *Daddy*, relax," I couldn't keep a straight face.

"Relax?" he repeated as his right eye twitched causing my smile to spread. "I gotcho relax!" Carter quickly flipped me on my back as I gasped, bouncing up a little from the mattress.

"Didn't you just tell me to be careful—"

"You a'ight," he blew it off, lifting my shirt over my belly as I giggled.

Kissing down the brown line on my stomach, I knew exactly where Carter was going with this and I couldn't be happier. The man wasn't just skilled with his hands and dick... His mouth did more than just talking. Licking my lips in anticipation, I caught Carter watching me with a ravenous grin.

"Oh, shit!" he cursed as he turned to the left where the digital clock sat on the bedside table. "Da Good Doctor finna come on!" Carter shot up, snatching the remote from the table as I lied back in shock.

"Carter, I know you're not serious—"

"Mani..." he groaned as I slowly propped myself up on my elbows, seeing the thrill in his eyes as the TV light flickered against his orbs. "I'ma do you right—I promise," he told me and I knew there wouldn't be any convincing him—*Wait a minute!*

Crawling beside him, his eyes looked to me then back at the screen as my hand slid up his thigh, touching him through his sweats. Smirking, he swiped my hand away but I went back for the kill.

"C'mon, Mani, chill—"

"You're the one who got me started," I told him as I squeezed his dick through the fabric causing him to shudder and grin. "Just a quickie—"

"No."

"Please!" I begged, poking my lip out as Carter paused the TV to look at me. "See, you paused it—"

"So I wouldn't miss shit—"

"And we have DVR!" I called him out as he threw his head back laughing. "So you can just record it and watch—"

Jumping off the bed, Carter gripped both my legs, pulling me towards the edge as I laughed. Yanking my panties off forcefully, I could see the little boy in him pissed off that he didn't get to watch what he wanted but I knew the freak in Carter wanted to slide inside just as much as I wanted to feel him.

"Should've neva turned yo ass out," he mumbled as I giggled while he spread my legs apart. "Can't neva do what I wanna do—"

"Shut up and do me!"

Looking up from between my legs his face was playfully serious. Trying to close my legs, Carter held them open as I continued laughing. Giving me one last glare, my husband dipped down and got to work. *My husband! I love it here!*

CHAPTER SIX

Carter

I used to go out to parties
And stand around
Cuz I was too nervous
To really get down...

TAPPING MY GREAT AUNT PEARL ON THE SHOULDER, SHE looked up smiling. Eyes watering and blue from age, she lifted her hands to be embraced. My daddy's oldest living relative, Aunt Pearl was pushing 93 and still kicking it. Moving around without her cane and even shuffled her feet and hands to the music playing. Enveloping her shaky arms around me, I kissed her stubbled cheek as she cooed and giggled, squeezing me tighter with each chuckle.

"You know you get handsomer and handsomer the more I see you, *Carl*," she told me as we broke our embrace. "I tell Peachy she's been blessed," her eyes danced around my face as I smiled. "And those dimples," she was confusing me with Troy, again. "Smile for me, so I can see em!" she pinched my cheeks causing me to cheese harder.

"Aunt Pearl, you keep mixin' me up wit Troy," I told her as she nodded her head.

"Who now?" her face scrunched up in confusion.

"My cousin—David's second boy?" I tried stroking her memory as she nodded slowly, probably still confused.

"Solomon and David?" She asked me as I nodded. "Yeah—I remember them... *Ooo*, you look just like Solomon," she told me something I'd heard all my life as I grinned and nodded my head.

"Dats my daddy—"

"Sure is!" Her high-pitched voice tickled me pink as we both chuckled together. "You remember yo grandaddy, Abel?" she asked me as I nodded my head, again. "*Mmhmm*... You look like him—Hair slicked down, jet black—You gotta relaxer?"

Doubling over in laughter, I shook my head as the perplexed look on Aunt Pearl's face cracked me up even more.

"Yeah... Issa perm," I lied as her eyes rounded.

It was better to lie than to keep explaining myself to Aunt Pearl. She might've still be kicking it but I think her memory loss was a sign that my cousin Pat needed to get her checked out. Not being one to speak things up on people but catching dementia in its early stages could slow the process.

"I'ma finna make my rounds, Auntie," I kissed her cheek again she squeezed me giggling. "Thank you for comin'," I said as we broke our embrace.

"Oh, I wouldn't miss it baby," she told me grinning from ear-to-ear.

Walking away from Aunt Pearl, I scanned the heads in attendance until I found the one I was looking for. Amani was warm like the rays from the sun. A still pond, calm and serene. Earth when viewed from space. My morning and nightly prayers... More than just a breath of fresh air. I could simply say she was my peace, but she was much more and I never went a day without telling her, just that. Yeah, I joked and teased the hell out of her but you could ask Amani what she meant to me and she'd be able to deliver a ten-page thesis with quotes, links, and dates of when, where, how, and what was told to her. Watching her, swollen with my child, interacting with my mama and aunties... I couldn't dream up a better picture. Slipping my hands into my pockets, I was ready to shout my love for her from the mountain tops.

For Amani to not like crowds or being put on the spot, she was handling the camaraderie surrounding her belly quite well. Yeah, a baby shower is for the baby but it's about the parents—Especially the mother. She was hugging and interacting with people she'd never met a day in her life. Mostly people from my family that my mama introduced her to... But Amani was cooler than I usually am in most situations. Shawty taking shit so well, I might just have the DJ cut the music and hop on the mic. But Amani would probably kill me with her glare. *Shit, I might just do it before everybody leave,* I told myself just as Troy came through the entrance with Yelly. He spotted me a second after he arrived, pulling Yelly close to whisper in her ear as I watched her nod and scan the heads in attendance. After the way she held shit down last year, I'd never be able to look at her the same. She was truly my nigga's equal, and I was finally happy about them being together.

"*Bubba*, gotta notha baby comin'," Troy shook up with me as I chuckled and shook my head. "And just in time—"

"Don't tell me ya'll bout to bring anotha—"

"Nah... Well, I'on know," Troy shrugged like it was nothing as I laughed at him. "Dats da wife so it is what it is," he spoke just like I had to Amani.

She didn't understand the way the men in my family viewed shit. We came from two-parent homes and wanted to continue that tradition. Especially since we were known to bring more men into this world than women. And I didn't just trying to tie the knot just so Cairo could fall under the same umbrella as his sister... He was going to have that regardless— That's why I kept him around my parents. So he could see more than destruction and hoodrat shit. I wanted Amani carrying my name because she deserved it. And she didn't think so—That's the main reason. After listening to her troubled childhood and how crazy and negligent her mama was... Raising her daughters like a pack of wolves—Nah, I couldn't even call em that because even wolves had a sense of pride within their pack. To bring their young up to take over what they started. Now, I didn't like her speaking ill of the dead but I wasn't going to allow the shit Jewel instilled into Amani to become her reality. She was more than a doormat—She had potential and showcased just how resilient and intelligent she was. *Shit, my baby was bad all by her damn self.*

"Ya'll know what ya'll havin'—Whatchu doin'?" Troy's questions pulled me from my thoughts as my bottom lip hung open, slightly confused. "Yo ass in love—"

"You just now noticin' dat shit?" Collin came from behind me, shaking up with Troy just as Desmond casually walked up with his hands in his pockets and his wife beside him.

"Wussup, Bilan," I pulled her slim fram into a hug as she giggled softly.

"Hey, cousin," she kissed the side of my face before smudging her thumb against my cheek, probably to wipe her lipstick off. "Congrats, to you, two—*Mommy* is so beautiful and pleasant," she said while eyeing Troy who looked to his brother then back at me before smirking and shaking his head.

"Whatchu laughin' at?" I asked what Desmond wanted to but didn't.

"Nothin'," Troy chose to keep the family drama at bay as he shook his head, looking off to the other faces in attendance.

He and Troy were still on the fence with one another but not like it was before. It was more guilt than anything. Especially from Desmond who, like me, thought he had Yelly pegged. We didn't trust Troy's judgement, and it tore a rift between us like no other. And I used to wonder how Troy so easily came around for me and not Desmond, when Amani showed me a bigger image. She basically had to get me to see Troy as my cousin and not a brother—Granted he was my uncle's son but the way we were brought up together, it sometimes felt like Collin wasn't my only sibling. And if Collin ever crossed me like Desmond had Troy... I'd probably be salty around him too.

"Excuse me," Amani squeezed herself in between Collin and Troy to get to me. "Hey, *brother* Troy," Amani teased Troy who smirked and hugged her. "Desmond..." she hugged him too before smiling up at Collin. "Collin—"

"Baby sis!" My brother grabbed Amani's left hand, pulling her over to him before scrunching up his face to glance down at her hand in his. "Da fuck is dis?" he questioned me and Amani whose lips were twisting as she looked over at me for an answer.

"We, *uh*..." I stammered as Troy, Desmond, and Ebony's focus was on the bling on Amani's finger.

"Oh, my gosh—You're engaged?" Ebony gushed, throwing her arms around Amani who giggled and shook her head.

"Married—"

"*What?*" Everybody encircling us spoke at once.

"*Excuse me?*" I heard my mama's voice as I huffed, causing Collin to giggle. "Hold on, Peggy," she shushed her sister to come over to our huddle. "Did I just hear you say *married*?" she knows what she heard.

"Yeah—"

"Carter Solomon Banks!"

"Ma, quit bein' dramatic," I smacked my lips as the rest of the guys laughed at me.

"I'm being dramatic because my son tied the knot, and I wasn't privy to it?" She clutched the pearls around her neck as my father walked up, standing behind her. "Solomon, do you hear this?" My mama turned over her shoulder, throwing my dad into the conversation as he looked to me pitifully.

"*Say*, mama, c'mon—It wasn't even like dat," I groaned, hating that the vibe had shifted from pleasant camaraderie to attacking me.

"Are ya'll married or not?" Her eyes shifted towards Amani who immediately hung her head in shame. "Then it is like that," she turned towards me as I grinned from being put on the spot. "Pam, did you know about this?" she called on Troy and Desmond's mama who was shaking her head, just as clueless as my mama's sisters standing around her. "Peggy? Susie? Rach?"

"Granny knew," I cut her investigation short as two of my aunts, along with my mama gasped.

"Just like mama to do something like this!" My mama's eyes cinched in my direction as me and Collin looked at each other before doubling over. "Carter and Collin, I don't think ya'll wanna mess with me right now!" Was my mama's way of threatening us but never worked as we laughed even harder.

Going to the next extreme, Megan Banks started swinging on me and my brother. Just like old times, except it didn't hurt, and we laughed until my daddy pulled her back.

"*Eh*, chill, ma—You gon' hit Mani!" I snickered as she huffed and puffed, holding her right hand in the air to whack me across my shoulders with, again.

"I should!" she snapped her neck to the side when Amani was still standing. "But I know you put her up to it—"

"*Wait*—Well, hol'up!" My face had confusion written all over it. "Why you always blamin' me?" I beckoned as my mama lowered her hand. "Mani wanted my last name—Otherwise I woulda took hers—"

Both Amani and my mama hit me as I laughed.

"*Eh*, I believe dat shit," Collin added his two cents as I smacked my lips waving him off. "Dis nigga not just in love—His ass *smitten*," Collin had the whole hall laughing after that. "Look at his cheeks—Rosey in blush," Collin flicked the side of my face as I hit him back, laughing because my lick wasn't as hard as usual because I couldn't stop laughing. "*My baby havin' my baby*,—Head ass." Collin mocked me as the room erupted in laughter.

In the midst of all the laughing, I could see the hurt displayed on my mama's face as I threw my left arm around her neck. It was never my intention to exclude anyone but I couldn't ignore the moment me, Mani, and Granny experienced together. If it made her feel better, Mani, and I were already in talks of throwing a traditional church wedding, so both families could partake in.

"We're going to have a formal ceremony with the rest of the families," Amani spoke my thoughts before me as she inched closer to my mama and me. "It was an *in the moment* kind of thing—Like, I don't even think we put much thought into what we were really doing—"

"So why get married, then?" Collin scoffed as Ebony slapped her hand across his chest. "What?"

"Because—Nigga…" I spat at my brother who was smirking tauntingly, "Whether we got married a week ago or weeks from now—It doesn't *negate* da fact dat we still love each other."

"*Aww,*" a few of the women cooed as I bashfully dropped my head, smiling.

"Ain't no *aww*—Negate my ass," Collin shot back at me as we laughed, shoving each other like old times.

"Well, either way…" My mama kept up the theatrics. "I still would've liked to have been there—"

"Me too," Aunt Rachel tossed in, like a baby sister would.

"Ya'll will," I cut my eyes at my mama's baby sister, as she giggled and shrugged.

Six years older than me, for the first five years of my life I thought she was my big sister. My mama used to have Rachel every other week and every day in the summer. We were so close, at times, I didn't properly address her… Some days she was Auntie other days she was just Rachel.

"It better be right after this baby is born," my mama pointed her small round finger in my face as I grinned and nodded my head.

"Not right after—"

"Carter don't play with me," she cut me off causing me and the rest of the guys to laugh.

"A'ight—But I ain't got no control ova Mani's healin' process," I reminded my mama as her face soften as she turned to look over at Amani.

"Okay… Well, soon," my mama changed her expectations as Amani nodded her head in agreement. "Six weeks, after we'll be fitting you in your dress!" she happily clasped her hands together as my mama's sisters came to Amani's side.

"Yay!" I joined in happiness, squeezing my mama, Mani, Rachel, and whoever else I could in my arms.

BUZZZ!

My phone vibrated in my pocket as I broke the embrace to retrieve it. Surprised to see my son calling me, I backed further away from everybody to answer it.

"Daddy, I'm outside," Cairo said before I could get a word out.

"Whatchu mean—Outside da venue?" I needed him to clarify.

"Yeah—My mama dropped me off," he sounded excited.

"A'ight, hol'up—I'll be back," I told Mani as she and my mama slowly nodded their heads, confused about where I was running off to.

Shuffling towards the double doors, I let myself out. Standing in front of Dede's Lexus, Cairo had on the fit I'd picked out for him. A Burberry button up and white dress pants. The typical hood baby shower attire.

"My man," I clapped my hands together as he popped his collar and turned to the side so I could see the fade from the side. "Already—I see you boy!" I chuckled as I got close enough to pull him into a hug.

Sweeping my hand over his waves a few times to flatten his hair a little, I could hear him laughing. Goofy like his uncle, I looked up from my son to see Dede watching us. Nodding my head once to acknowledge her she did the same, giving me a weak smile. Since our first court hearing, De'Asia and I have been to three more, and I was seeing tremendous progress and growth from her. Shawty wasn't as dependent on me and she even got the Lexus truck all on her own—*Well...* half from the money I was dropping into her account and the other from her EKG funds.

Dede buckled down, took an eleven week course, gotta

certificate and was now working at the hospital, monitoring hearts. Something I took pride in telling because I loved seeing her overcome every obstacle that was set in place to hinder her from the potential I knew she had in her.

"Congratulations," Dede told me as she dangled a gift bag from her window.

"Thank you," I bowed my head as I stepped up to retrieve the bag.

"No problem," she told me as we stared for a moment longer before hearing the door crank open. "You can keep him for the weekend—He's excited and I wanna get some rest cuz I gotta work in da morning," Dede told me as I nodded my head, tightening the grip around my son's neck as he snickered.

"Wussup, Dede," Collin got closer to the truck to shake up with her.

"Hey, Lin—When you gon' pop a few out?"

"Next year—"

"Shut yo ass up," I chuckled with the both of them as I shook my head. "You know Eb ain't goin' for none of dat shit, right now," I snickered as Collin shrugged and nodded.

Opening his mouth to speak, Collin stopped as he kept his eyes to the left. Following his gaze, several black trucks had rolled up behind Dede. Off instinct, me and my brother reached behind us as I pushed Cairo behind me. Cocking that thang, a widow rolled down to reveal an ice-glaring Arab. Clenching my jaw, it hit me... *I know why dis muhfucka is here.* Lowering my weapon and smiling, Collin followed suit.

"I mean if you wanna buss and bang shots, lez go!" Tyrone leaned out the back window as the smile on my face spread.

"Nigga," I laughed as I swiped my hand down my face, walking up to the first truck. "Don't be poppin' up unannounced—"

"We called Troy—Where he at?" Torin cut his brother off as I pointed to the building to see the double doors opening.

"Wussup," Troy filed through with Delando and Desmond behind him.

"Why you ain't tell cuzzo we was comin'?" Tyrone yelled back at Troy as he stepped out the truck, helping his wife get out.

"Cuz I ain't want his lovey dovey ass to ruin da surprise for his *wife*—"

"*Wife?*" Salimah's eyes bugged out as Tyrone smacked his lips down at her. "Don't—*Tsk!* Hush!"

"Nah, you hush—"

"Did you and my sister get married?" Salimah asked me as I nodded my head. "And y'all didn't think to invite *us*?" she circled her little finger around herself, Ty and whoever was still getting out the trucks.

"We ain't have da weddin' yet—"

"Lima, please!" Fatima came over to the curb with rolling her eyes. "Like the way you and Ty skipped off to Vegas—You should be the last person complaining!"

"That wasn't even..." Salimah clasped her mouth closed as everybody started laughing.

"I told you..." Ty shook his head as Salimah rolled her eyes to the side with a grin on her face.

"Carter—OH MY GOSH!" Amani came out the door screaming as she ran to get to her sisters.

Jumping and screaming, we watching all three of them huddle and hug each other like they hadn't seen each other in years. I mean, it's been a few months but by the way they FaceTime and call each other... They shouldn't be acting like this.

"Look at you!" Fatima pulled back from her two sisters to palm Amani's belly. "I can't believe you were the last one to have a baby," she giggled as Amani shrugged.

"I know—Backwards how the baby sister was first—"

"And got the most kids," Salimah chimed in as Fatima smacked her lips before grinning.

"Well, now we're all mothers and that's what matters most!" Fatima pulled Amani back into a hug as the smile on my baby's face brightened. "We need a summer home down here, *Joseph*!" Fatima was already jumping the gun as Torin shook his head, smirking while we laughed at him.

"They gon' visit us—"

"Not when the baby's first born and I wanna be here for that!" Fatima's voice was whiny but stern as Torin exhaled, knowing his ass was going to give into whatever she asked him for.

"Me too!" Salimah giggled as Tyrone rolled his eyes to the side. "And we will!"

"Yeah, you keep talkin—"

"Let's go inside!" Salimah cut Tyrone off as the sisters locked arms, leaving us on the pavement.

"Damn, I guess we just chopped liver," Travis stood beside Torin with his arm slung over Trita's neck.

"Aw, damn, wussup Trita," I spoke to her not even realizing she had been here the whole time.

"Hey, Carter—Don't even trip... I know your wife doesn't really know me," she shrugged as I smirked, knowing Amani didn't really care for Trita because Fatima told her how snotty she was towards her.

"Yeah, dassit," I told her as we hugged.

"A'ight, Carter—Cairo, you be good," Dede alerted me to her presence again, as I chucked my chin up as she pulled off.

"Who dat is?" Torin asked.

"Baby mama—"

"Aww—Das yo mama," Torin pointed to my son who was

grinning and nodding. "Wussup, lil man!" He shook up with Cairo, and I watched his brothers do the same.

"None—Just chillin'," Cairo cooly replied as Torin and his brother laughed.

"Yeah, I see—Keepin' dem grades up, I hope."

"*Already!*" My son sounded just like me as we chuckled at him.

Heading back inside, the sound of another car pulling up turned me around. Squinting as I scanned the body, I'd never seen this car before. *Man, who da fuck is dis?* I thought as the back door opened.

"Did y'all miss me?" Dree, Amani's brother got out with his hands in the air.

"Yo ass!" Collin laughed as he shook his head.

"What?" Dree coughed just before the skunk hit my nose.

This muhfucka couldn't go nowhere without smoking... And I wasn't one to talk because I used to be like that too. Shit, Mani too. But with her being pregnant and quitting cold turkey, I hadn't smoked as much as I used to. The last time I faced a blunt was a week ago, and that was only to keep my emotions on guard after hearing about Granny. Before that, I think me, and Troy smoked while I was at his crib talking and that was about a month ago.

"Amani know I'm here?" Dree asked as he walked with us into the venue.

"Nah—"

"YADRIEL?" Amani spotted him as she ran over to him.

"Wussup, Mani Mon," Dree held his arms open until Amani reached him.

"Oh my..." Amani blinked twice off contact.

Yeah, dat muhfucka is strong, I thought as I chuckled with everybody near us.

"Get off my wife, nigga—You bouta to fuck her up," I told Dree as I pulled Amani away from him while they laughed.

"*Wife?* Damn, congrats—Bro and Sis!" Dree ignored my request, hugging Mani again as she giggled. "I can't wait to tell everybody," he was genuinely excited but I could see Amani's face and knew she was wondering why her father didn't come. "You know pops sends his love and I know he gon' be happy as hell to hear dis news," Dree told Amani as she nodded her head slowly.

Watching her, I didn't see Salimah creeping up behind Amani. Grabbing her arm, she smirked over at Dree and I could feel the heat even as she showed her teeth. There was something there, and it wasn't good.

"I'm gonna steal *my* sister away," Salimah spoke with her brows as Dree nodded, blowing his whole high.

Not saying a word as Amani and Salimah rejoined Fatima, Yelly, and Ebony, Dree still had this stupid look on his face. Collin came over, squatting down in front of me and Dree, picking something off the floor.

"Here, nigga," He blew into the palm of his hand. "I think I got most of yo face off da floor—"

Throwing my head back with the rest of my niggas, we all shared a laugh at Dree's expense. I missed this shit!

"Eh, man, fuck y'all—Why yo wife don't like me?" Dree asked Tyrone as he shrugged it off.

"Once I find out, I'll letchu know," he told him but I had a feeling Ty already knew why and was trying to distance himself from the drama.

Despite Dree being a cool ass nigga, Salimah was his wife. The first player on his team and you didn't fuck up your home over bro code. That shit was dead after you hit twenty. Don't believe me, ask them niggas doing football jersey numbers in the pen or the homies taking dirt naps... You stay loyal but not at the expense of the woman you sleep next to at night. She the hardest player on your team.

Using this as my cue to walk away, I made my way back over to my wife. She was still smiling, glowing as she shared this moment with her sisters and closest friends. Shanae from school even came through.

"Oh, my gosh!" Salimah squealed as she looked from Amani to Fatima. "This used to be our song!"

"Y'all song?" Tyrone and Torin spoke together.

Leaning in close enough to Amani's ear, she was playing coy.

"Dis was y'all song?" I whispered as she grinned and shrugged, nibbling on my bottom lip.

> *He might be doin' you*
> *But he's thinkin' about me*
> *So lay that finger on another lover*
> *And go find another brother*

"*I know he's my man!*" Ebony sang with Salimah as they both giggled.

"*He's all in my hands—It's feels good when he calls my name. Dontcha wish ya had the same?!*" Salimah swirled around as Fatima and Amani continued their shy girl act.

The cat was already out the bag. Knowing Amani was probably a little ass girl singing this song. *So, Shawty been fast.* Nudging her towards her sister, Amani giggled and elbowed me.

"Don't act shy now," I told her as Torin laughed, pushing Fatima forward, too. "Dis y'all song!"

"No—We just—"

"Mani, now you know—"

"Shut up!" Amani quickly shushed her little sister as she giggled, clamping her lips closed.

"Y'all was bad as hell," Torin flicked Fatima's earlobe as she giggled and shrugged.

"You love it," she responded as he nodded, causing a few of us, who saw him, to laugh.

"Shit, every night—"

"*Joseph!*" Fatima gripped his arm, but it was already too late.

We heard him and we were already laughing. Enjoying the company of family and close friends, I think Amani's baby shower was a hit. Shit, Shawty ain't stopped grinning since we walked in this hoe. And I'm cool if she's happy.

CHAPTER SEVEN

Amani

Pressing my finger on the period button, a huge weight lifted off my shoulders. This was it, the last paper I'd ever write for this class. In less than two months, I'd have my bachelors and although I'd wanted this degree since I signed up two years ago... Knowing I wouldn't be able to walk overshadowed my accomplishment. I mean, not too many people could say they've come as far as I but I wanted the whole experience. When late April, early May came, my class would be celebrating, and I'd be home with a newborn—Well, a month old baby, I know Carter wouldn't feel comfortable allowing me to take out just to hear my name being called so I could walk across a stage.

Closing my laptop, I sighed, knowing everything was aligned and there wasn't much else to do. My sense of purpose was diminishing until I signed up for my masters. *Hmm, maybe I could start my masters online and next year take a couple classes—*

"Whatchu gotta taste for?" Carter always came in when I was feeling down, like he had a sensor that clicked in his head.

Shrugging, I didn't want to eat anything but the fruit his mama sent over, weekly, after she found out I'd been craving pineapples like no other. Pushing myself off the bed, I waddled towards the bathroom, knowing Carter was hot on my trail. Sitting on the toilet, I counted to ten and got to six when Carter finally came in after me.

"Wus wrong witchu?" he asked as I lifted my shoulders, again, hearing him exhale. "Mani—"

Bursting into tears, my bottom lip quivered as my eyes leaked the pitiful thoughts inside my head. Per my own experience and the exerts from the pregnancy books... Crying was one of the many things I loathe about being pregnant. I couldn't hide any of my emotions.

"I'm finished," I sobbed as Carter came over to me, squatting down so his eyes were level to mine.

"Finished with what?" His patience was commendable because whenever I got like this, he'd always fish for answers in an attempt at making me feel better.

"My last term paper," I sounded and probably looked like the biggest baby on earth as I swiped the tears from my cheeks, catching the smirk on Carter's face. "It's not funny!"

"It kinda is—"

"Stop—Get off me!" I sobbed, pushing him back with a roll of my eyes, causing Carter to fall on his butt.

With him laughing at me, I didn't have the urge to cry anymore. Instead, I wanted to do more than push him. That's usually how my moods switched but under the guise of pregnancy, these swings happened quicker and quite often.

"What?" Carter's face tightened up as he crouched back on his feet.

Rolling my eyes and wiping myself, I wasn't in the mood for his playing around. He knew how I got and yet; he chose to make matters worse with his teasing.

"Do whatchu finna do—"

"Stop, Carter!" I groaned as he got behind me as I moved to the sink to wash my hands.

"Or what?" he challenged as his nose tickled the side of my face.

Looking at me through the mirror, I kept the frown on my face as I cut the water and dried my hands. Waiting until my hands were dry enough, Carter snatched the towel from my hands, tossing it into the sink bowl, before yanking me into him. Stumbling as I fell into his arms, I chuckled a little making him laugh too.

"Stop doing that—"

"What I'm doin', Shawty?" Carter was playing dumb as my jaw twitched and my eyes shifted to the left. "Look at me," he demanded, but I refused, hearing him chuckle lowly. "Mani," he called my name in an attempt to get me to cooperate but I remained defiant. *"Every time I see yo face it makes me wanna —Sing and every time I think about ya love it drives me —CRAZAYYY!"*

"Must you always sing?" I complained, cutting into his solo as I fought the urge to crack a smile.

"I hold da key to yo heart! And nobody loves you like I dooo!" Carter changed Rome's song to fit the level of annoyance he was causing me. *"Onlay wanna be witchu..."* Carter

rolled his hips seductively as I burst into laughter. "*I belong to youuu—*" He shook me gently, as he swayed around the room. "*I give all my love-uhveee to youuu!*"

Pecking his lips as he leaned into my face, I could go for a quickie and I knew it didn't take much convincing with Carter, either. Still, I wanted it to be fun, so I dipped my hands into his sweats, feeling him shudder as he held me. Gripping his dick as he continued to sway back and forth, knowing Carter, he would make me pull it out before he got to work.

"You just gon' play wit it—"

"Hush," I snickered as the warmth from my hands and his dick had the palm of my hands sweaty. "I'm trying to get it out," I told him as I struggled with his waistband for a second longer.

"I know I'm packin' but you—"

Sighing loudly, I cut into whatever he was trying to say, making him laugh as I freed the monster. Nothing like vitamin D well into the night. The best form of medicine, if you ask me.

"Since you got allat attitude, I'm finna make you ride *it*," Carter told me as I giggled and shrugged. "*Ah-hee-hee-hell...*" he mocked me, making his small attitude all the funnier. "Okay," Carter nodded his head up and down as he pulled the both of us out of the bathroom towards the bed. "I'on wanna hear no winded pleas for me to hit it from da back—"

"Shut up!" I snorted in laughter. "*Winded?* You better not be callin' me fat—"

"Call em like I see—"

SLAP!

Smacking him silent, Carter quickly hemmed me up. It wasn't a hard hit, but I knew the only way to shut him up was doing the very thing he hated. Putting my hands on Carter was a no-no, but I was not about to let him trample all over my emotions by calling me fat. Jokingly or not... He knew better. I'm sensitive enough, as is.

"Mani, I'm bout to fuck you up!" He growled as his grip around my shirt tightened.

"*Fuck* it up, daddy," I cooed moving his hand down towards my belly.

"Say, man—Quit playin'!" Carter groaned like I knew he would, causing me to giggle.

"*What*—Carter, *this* created *this*," I pointed to my stomach as he smacked his lips, shaking his head. "A couple months ago, you were all for it—"

"I'm not tryna hear none of dat shit, man!" Carter was sick, and I was enjoying every moment of it. "My dick went limp soon as you did dat shit—"

"And you act like you want a house chalk-full of babies—"

"I do—"

"So *whatchu waitin' fah*?" I mimicked his way of speaking to a T, seeing the corners of his mouth turn up as my eyes dropped to his exposed genitals.

I don't care what he was feeling; I was ready to let off some steam. Even if I had to do all the work... Even though I didn't want to. Which I probably wouldn't, for too long, because once Carter was in his element, he'd take charge and the rest... *Lawd, that's what I'm yearning to feel!*

"So, you gon' rape me... In front of my son?" He asked as I immediately flushed white, looking past him towards the door. "Whatchu—*Ahhh!*" Carter pointed in my face laughing. "Dats whatcho ass get—Cairo ain't here!"

Pushing him away from me as he regained control of the situation, Carter grabbed my arms again as I tried getting on the bed. He was still laughing and being his regular annoying self.

"*Freaky ass!*"

"Shut up..." I curled my toes as I rolled my eyes to the side. "Are we gonna do this or what—"

"Shit, what else you finna do?" Carter was being cocky now as I tilted my head to the side, blinking.

"You must not be familiar with my options, *baby daddy*," I batted my eyes as the last two words slipped from my lips, causing him to chuckle in shock.

"I gotcho *baby daddy*," Carter's gruff tone sent waves of lust down my spine as he pulled me into him.

Standing in between my legs, his face was nestled deep into the crook of my neck, trailing kisses. Soft, wet, and sensual. Moaning as he continued toying with my emotions, sometimes I just wanted him to get to the point. Foreplay was fun, and it did add that extra humph but... Unexpected, unrehearsed sex did have its perks.

"You changed yo name—"

"Yes!" I groaned, causing him to chuckle.

"Lemme see!" He challenged, pulling away from me as I giggled, gazing flatly into his green eyes.

"Are you serious, right now?" I asked, blinking slowly as Carter nodded his head. "You want me to open my laptop, log into blackboard and show you my name is changed?"

"*Yes*," Carter cut me off more anxious and obnoxious than before as I pushed him further away from me, hearing him laugh about it.

"Fine," my lips were pursed together as I hopped off the bed to retrieve my laptop.

Hidden in the bedside table drawer, I pulled it out and opened it. Typing my password, his name and birthday, to unlock it then clicking Safari. Taking ten-seconds to load my school website was the last tab open before I logged out. Moving the cursor to the appropriate links, it took ten more seconds to pull up my transcripts. Shocking me as the name *Amani Monroe Banks* headed the top of the page, I couldn't stop the smile spreading across my face. *There is was... In writing.* My name for the rest of my life.

Pecking my lips gently, Carter smiled in between kisses as I playfully giggled, exchanging a kiss for every one he gave me. Blindly closing my laptop again, it didn't even matter what was said before this moment.

"Let's role play," Carter broke away to say this. "You be my wife and I'll be—"

"How is that role playing?" I giggled as I watched him pull his shirt over his head, shrugging. "I'm already your wife—"

"*Ooo*, I love to hear it!" he shivered as I laughed even more. "*Let's play a lil game, my forte. Here's a little fantasy and role—*"

"Carter," I called out his name sternly as he laughed in the middle of his song.

"A'ight," he smacked his lips, tugging on my sweats. "Take deez shits off!" he ordered as I pouted, not feeling like getting back out of bed again to take them off. "*Tsk!* Lazy ass," he grumbled yanking and pulling on the legs of my sweats as I giggled. "Turn around," he ordered once he got them off.

"I gotta—"

"Nah, you ain't gotta do shit but face da board," he pointed towards the headboard as I grinned and turned over slowly. "Allat back talk finna add up to deez back shots," Carter mumbled behind me as the palm of his hand slapped against my butt.

"*Sss*, not so hard," I hissed as Carter shook his head pointing towards the board.

Giggling and rolling my eyes as I turned back around, I could hear him quietly snickering as I waited for him to do something.

"*Cuz I'm yo master and you're my slave. Everything I say,*

you will obey, yeah!" he sang as I fought the urge to turn back around. *"Playing my little game of role play pretend, yeahh-eh-eh-eh-aw-yeahhh!"*

"Carter, I swear to God—"

SLAP!

I know my right cheek was red because it stung after contact with his palm.

"Whatchu say?" he asked pulling my panties to the side. "*Huh?*"

"Stop—"

"Nah, what I tell you—"

"Okay—"

"Quit talkin' ova me," Carter talked over me as his fingers slipped in, between, and around my second set of lips.

Breathing slowly, I knew I was wet enough for insertion but the longer he toyed with my clit the more my heartbeat raced building up my anticipation. Licking my lips, I closed my eyes because in a minute; I was about to turn around and pummel Carter. Pulling his fingers from inside of me, I heard him sucking as I bit down on my bottom lip to keep from giggling too loudly. *Carter is such a freak.* Gripping my sides as he hummed out the rest of Role Play he removed one hand and finally eased himself inside.

"*Ahhh,*" my jaw dropped with sweet relief.

Grabbing the back of my neck, Carter took his word seriously and proceeded to pound every bit of attitude I'd displayed earlier out of me. Thus the reason for always copping one in the first place. Carter's stroke was addictive, to say the lease. Even before I was sure he knocked me up. He had the Midas touch because my honey pot was oozing liquid gold with each stroke. If there was a way, I'd let him impregnate me again during my current pregnancy. I don't even care—

"*Ooo... Wait—AHHH!*" My knees quaked as my bottom lip quivered.

Giving in wasn't one of my strongest suits, even though I've done so in the past but I don't think I'd be able to take another orgasm on all fours. Digging my nails into the comforter, I squeezed to combat the pleasure urges to collapse. Using my breathing techniques from my Lamaze class... *In through the nose and out the mouth*—Which I should've already been doing since this was the proper way of breathing. Arching my back and rocking with each motion. Of course my movements paired with Carter's only created more friction but those same movements somehow gave me Megan's knees and I was able to keep my body up. *Oh God!*

SLAP!

"*CARTER!*"

"*I know whatchu thinkin'!*" He laughed as my left cheek and face burned with passion.

"No, you—*Ooo, okay!*" I breathed as he rolled his pelvis into me, grinding slowly.

"*Yeah...*" his voice was deep, vibrating through me the same way the bass from a speaker would if you stood too close to it. "*Mhmm*—Dis whatchu wanted, remember?" he sneered, snaking one of his arms underneath my stomach to get between my legs. "*Fuck it up, Daddy*—Dats whatchu told me to do, Mani. I'm just doin' whatchu want—*Mmm!*"

"*AH—Uh-Ahh, yeah!*"

My eyes were rolling to the back of my head as he kept the same rhythm and tempo. Hearing his low humming grow in volume, I assumed Carter knew the affect he was having on me, now. Satisfied to silence, the only thing I could do was pant, gasp, and occasionally *Ooo and Ah* when he hit a spot better than the last stroke.

"*Now, I can be yo Cowboy—*"

SLAP!

"*I can be yo dancer baby, Ooo, yeah—*"

SLAP!

Carter sung as sweat dripped from his body onto mine. Keeping a tight grip on my hips, even if I wanted to topple over, I wouldn't. He had everything under control. No matter how off-key or annoying... He kept it going and this song would be added to the list of songs he imprinted into my brain long after sex was finished.

"*Ssshiitt*—I feel you, Shawty... Cum for me," Carter's strokes quickened and banged, slapping the front of his thighs into the back of mine.

Freezing completely, I don't think my movements mattered at this point. Another climax was peaking, and Carter was about to explode, himself. We'd done this enough times for me to know when he was ready. Still, he never finished without giving me that last blowout—

"*Ahhhhh—*"

"*Shit*—Yeah, yeah, yeah..." Carter hunched over me, releasing my sides as my face fell into the blankets.

Bursting, quivering, slobbering and screaming, all my energy was channeled. Tensing up from the shoulders down, I could feel Carter's dick jerking as he let go inside of me. Something he claimed was the best feeling in the world. Not having to pull out. Releasing the deepest sigh, I could feel Carter pulling out of me as I rolled over to my side.

"*Mmm*—Whatchu doin'?" Carter palmed my butt as I glanced up at him, feeling like I could sleep for days now. "We ain't done," he moved in and out of me slowly as I tried backing away from him, ending up flat on my back.

Too weak and starting to feel where he was coming from, I lazily lied there and took it. Leaning most of his weight into me, my eyes rolled to the back of my head and he hovered over me. Kissing my jawline down my neck as he stroked, I was ready to explode for the second time. Feeling Carter turn me on my side, he somehow maneuvered behind me without pulling out. Or maybe we've been like this—I don't know... It feels good either way.

"*Ooo—Oh my... Ahhh, didn't say it!*" I moaned as Carter lifted my leg, snickering into the crook of my neck.

"I know," he kissed my skin as I sucked on my button lip, still gripping the sheets. "But you wanted to—"

"You should be happy you make me feel like that," I told him, wincing from the pleasure.

"Nah," Carter's voice buzzed against my neck causing me to shiver.

This wasn't the sensation I needed at this moment. Trying to keep from shrieking, Carter sped up a little, digging as he wiggled inside of me. Tossing my head back, I grabbed the closest thing to me. His arm and squeezed, digging my nails into his skin as he groaned, face still nestled in the skin of my neck.

"Shit –*Mani*, damn!" Carter grunted as I loosened my grip, just a little, to ease some of his pain. "Yo ass should just cuss," he suggested as I closed my eyes, shaking my head. "Yeah—

C'mon," he kept his movements steady as I shook my head again. "I'ma show you—"

"No, *Carter,* no!" my voice wavered as he laughed at me.

"It's better than—"

"No, it's not!" I protested, wincing as a small squeak followed. *"Ooo—Okay... Maybe,"* I nodded my head causing Carter to chuckle.

Beating my back out from the side, silently, I could hear Carter laugh every couple seconds. *Did he—Ooo—Oh, my God, I think; Ahhh! Ooo, I should do it!* My thoughts were so scrambled I couldn't piece together what I thought I should be thinking. Closing my eyes as his strokes slowed and deepened, I could feel the leg he still held in the air quivering. Lowering my leg just enough to hook it over his arm, I could feel his fingers playing with my pearl as my body convulsed from the sensation. Pulling his face from my neck Carter lips brushed against my earlobe causing me to shudder, again. Biting it, gently, I scratched the hand he was using to play with my kitty as he stroked.

"*Shit*—Say it wit me," Carter instructed as I nodded my head. "*Nah, nah,*" he growled into my ear, "Say it!"

"Sss-*Uh*—"

"*Shit!*" he grunted as he pushed in and out of me.

"*Ssshiettt!*" I could feel liquid gushing as I released my inhibitions.

I've cursed before and have said worse than *shit* but I didn't make it a habit of doing so. My reasons weren't even based on morality nor religion because I didn't really believe in the latter. Was there a higher power? *Probably.* Did it guide me and keep me? *Maybe.* But I didn't make a habit out of talking outside of the time and space we could see or view through a telescope. Carter, on the other hand, never skipped a day without reminding me just how good God was. It actually made me laugh when he'd notice his talks flew in one ear and out the other. Not that it was intentional, but I wasn't raised like him. There wasn't Sunday service with the family followed by a huge Sunday dinner. Just thinking about it made me feel real southern—Country, even.

And if we went off the Christian spectrum... Carter flew way off the handle by living the life he was currently leading. Two children out of wedlock—Constant premarital sex... Well, not now but before, *God—Oops!* Okay... So maybe he was working in an effort to clean it up. With age comes a little wisdom. That's what I'll attribute that to—*What the fuck am I thinking? Oh, Shit, I did it*—SHIT! I DID IT AGAIN—

"SHIT!"

"Yeah—Just like dat!"

I could hear the smile in Carter's voice as he sped up the tempo a little. Like always, he got what he wanted from me.

"*Mmm...*" I didn't want to use up my new word, so I hummed and fought the urge to— "*AHHH—CARTER!*"

I fail every time. Every freaking' time!

"We got all night—"

"*Ugh!*" I groaned knowing he meant just that. "We can do it tomorrow—"

"Aw yeah... Tomorrow too," Carter agreed with me as we both laughed. "I got six weeks to make up for," he'd finally revealed why he was so much more friskier than before.

Dropping my shoulders as he helped moved me into the newest position, I couldn't even be mad at him. Six weeks was a long time to go from doing it almost every day—Two tines even to just nothing. And according to my little sisters your hormones are ten times worse after giving birth... And if you add breastfeeding, which I plan on doing, to the equation I'll be in hell.

"Okay—Let me ride it though," I offered as Carter released my leg, dropping to his back like he was one of Andy's toys.

Laughing at his silly self, I straddled his lap, grabbing him and sliding down. Tonight is going to be real nasty, sweaty, and worth every second.

CHAPTER EIGHT

Carter

"Nah, nah—Put dis shit right here!" Collin yelled at me as we both worked to set baby girl's crib up.

Since Amani fell asleep last night, my brother's been here setting the nursery up. We'd successfully bickered the whole time Collin put up the changing table and dresser. Picked at one another while folding and hanging up baby girl's clothes and just gone tit-for-tat until most of the boxes were opened, broken down and cleared out the room.

"When she due?" Collin asked me as he looked over all the pieces from the crib.

"Two weeks—"

"Damn," Collin whistled. "Dis shit been makin' me think about—"

"Don't even say dat shit," I cut my little brother off before he could speak a child into existence.

It's not that I didn't want him to experience the whims of fatherhood, I just didn't want him to base his decisions off me and everybody around him. Collin and Ray Ray didn't have children—Well, I'm not too sure about Ray Ray but he ain't had no surprise pop-ups so I'm gonna say he has no children. Still, they had plenty of time to decide. I didn't wait and I wish I would have. My son changed my life but I know I wasn't as prepared for him then as I am now with my baby girl. This pregnancy just feels different. And I could probably attest that to the fact that I love her mother. So much so that I married her—

"WHAT ARE YOU DOING!" Amani's voice boomed, knocking me from my thoughts. "NO, NO NO—CARTER!"

Watching my wife stomp over to the neatly stacked crib pieces, she started kicking the pile out of order as Collin shot up from the floor.

"What da fuck—MANI!" Collin called out to her, but she ignored him, still on her rampage. "CARTER!"

"Whatchu doin'?" I snatched Amani up as she was stomping towards him. "Stop—Hol'up, you a'ight?" I gripped her face, not liking that her chest was heaving and her fists were balled up.

"That's why you wanted me to go to bed!" she shrieked as my face scrunched up in confusion. "So you and your brother could go behind my back—"

"Yo, she delirious right now," Collin pointed at Amani who shot back a icy glare, getting the same from my little brother.

"I'm not delirious—You're just busted," Amani sassed as

Collin snorted in jest while I tried, like hell, not to laugh myself.

"*Busted*—Whatchu sayin', Shawty?"

"You can't put up the baby's crib!" Amani's arms waved frantically as I looked to my brother whose face had gone from amused to confused. "You can't put up the baby's crib or else the baby comes early!"

"What?"

"I'm not due for two more weeks—"

"And you'll have her when da time comes but Mani, I ain't finna be tryna figure dis shit out wit a screamin' baby in da house," I told her as she shook her head, not trying to hear me. "Dis bed finna go up—"

"NO!" Amani tried to go for the cherry wood piece she'd kicked near me but I blocked her. "Let me go!"

"Nah, chill out—"

"I am chill—"

"You not chill, Mani—Calm da fuck down cuz what's gon' make my baby come early is you kickin' and movin' and yellin' and shit!" I barked as inhaled and let it out slowly. "Relax, eh, bro," I turned over my shoulder to address Collin. "Just stop," I nodded once for him to know I didn't mean drop the project altogether but to break until I came back. "C'mon—"

"No, he's gonna build it if we leave—"

"I ain't touchin' shit, no moe," Collin assured Amani as I smirked and shook my head. "And I change my fuckin' mind—I ain't havin' no kids!" Collin made me laugh as Amani shot me a look.

"It's not funny—"

"I'm not laughin' atchu, *Shawty*, c'mon," I ushered Amani out of the nursery trying to keep my facial expression bleak.

Leading Amani back to our bedroom, I helped her back on

the bed and climbed in behind her. I thought for sure after the lovemaking we'd done she'd be knocked out for the night but I was wrong.

"Why you wake up?" I asked as she rested her head on my chest, yawning.

"I had to pee and you weren't here so I wanted to find you."

"You know I'm not goin' nowhere," I kissed the top of her head as her shoulders rose and fell. "Why you actin' like dat?"

"Because I can't sleep unless you're in the bed—"

"When dat shit start?" I wondered hearing her laugh.

"Since the third time you came to Chicago—"

"Before you moved down here?" I cut in to clarify as Amani nodded her head, giggling softly when I smacked my lips in disbelief. "Quit lyin'—"

"I'm not!" she whined as I smacked my lips again. "I really can't sleep without you—"

"Dats cuz yo ass was pregnant by then," I told her and now she was smacking her lips as I laughed. "You stay blamin' me like you ain't want it—"

"I did but you had an agenda—"

"*Tsk!* What agenda?" I played like she wasn't spitting facts.

Lifting her head from my chest so she could look me in the eyes, I burst into laughter as Amani grinned and rolled her eyes.

"I wasn't aimin' to getchu pregnant—"

"Just keep lying to me..." Amani sighed. "That's the best way to give this marriage longevity."

"Dis marriage gon' have longevity regardless," I told Amani as she shook her head. "So, you gon' leave me?"

"Yup—With all ten of our kids," Amani told me as I laughed with her. "I just can't do this anymore!" her voice changed in pitch as she acted out how she'd leave me.

"Shut up," I muffed the top of her head hearing her giggle. "I'ma leave yo as if you keep kickin' in doors and fuckin' shit up—"

"I did not kick in the door—It was already open!" Amani giggled as I groaned.

"Either way, you was on one," I told her as she shrugged. "Ain't no *I'on care*—You better care!"

"Well I don't!" Amani was trying to rile me up because she peered up at me then laughed once she noticed the stark gaze plastered on my face.

"Take yo ass to bed and shut up—"

"No, because you're just gonna go down the hall to finish up with Collin," she called my bluff as I shook my head, waving her off. "You can huff and puff all you want but I know—"

"Shut up, shut up, shut up!" I cut her off as she giggled. "You ain't right—I'm goin' to sleep too," I lied as Amani laughed even harder.

"No, you're not—"

"Mani!" My voice boomed over hers and I knew she was smiling. "You know what?" I lifted her head up so I could get up. "Face da board—"

"Stop!" Amani giggled as she propped the side of her face up on her hand.

"Nah, I'm for real—Get up," I grabbed her arm, pulling her up to me. "You got allat mouth let's put it to work!"

"Carter—"

"Face da fuckin' board," I told her as she poked her bottom lip out. "Mani, I'on feel no sympathy for you, Shawty... Turn around!"

"No—Okay, I'll go to bed!" she whined as I lifted my shirt over my head. "Too late—Date mouth just wrote a check I'm finna cash... And I want both ends," I winked as Amani doubled over in laughter.

"Nope just the mouth," she offered as I shook my head, dissatisfied with her suggestion. "You already—I'm a little sore," Amani pouted, referring to what we did a couple hours ago.

"It's a'ight—I'll go slow," I promised as she shook her head. "Don't worry, Shawty..." I told her as I turned her around, hearing her giggle. "You gon' learn to do what I tell you—"

"I won't!" Amani defiantly spat as I nodded my head.

"So it's gon' be face down ass up for da rest of our lives—I can live wit dat," I told Amani as I slapped her ass, making her laugh. "Take dis shit off!" I mumbled as I yanked her shorts, and panties down.

"Carter you better be gent—"

"You better face da board!"

SLAP!

"Okay!" Amani cried out as she turned back around.

SLAP!

"*Carter-ruh!*"

"You ain't gotta add extra syllables to my name—Dats dat attitude!" I told her as she giggled.

"I don't—"

"Dats three—"

"Carter, we're not doing this again!"

"Four," I hissed as I slid in.

"*Sss... Ahhh*," Amani breathed because she couldn't speak.

That's what I like to hear.

SCRATCHING the back of my head as my eyes scanned over the instructions, I was lost. In plain English, none of this shit looked right. I don't even think I had all the pieces needed to put this crib together. *Why da fuck did I get the convertible crib?*

"*Tsk!* Man—Gimme dis shit!" Collin stumbled up to his feet snatching the manual from my hands.

He'd always been the better mechanic out of the two of us. Just like our father, Collin could take anything apart and put it back together without ever having to see the instructions. If not for the family business, they'd be the poster people for a *Father & Son* type shop. I'd probably run the logistics—Making sure my father didn't undercut the supplier to keep costs down or keep Collin from buying the latest and greatest just because it was hot right now.

"Just make sure yo wife keep her ass in bed—"

"Eh, chill out," my brow rose letting Collin know that he was treading on thin ice talking about my baby.

"I'm just sayin'—Shawty was trippin'..." he chuckled as he shook his head. "I ain't neva heard no shit like dat in my life," he was still going as I rolled my eyes to the side, clenching my jaw.

Looking to the left of me and picking up the remote, I turned on the TV and scanned through the TV guide. Nothing was on this early in the morning, except reruns and infomercials. It was either the *Sham Wow* or *Good Times*. Sitting down in the rocking chair, I left my brother to do what he did better than me. Dozing off in the middle of my fifth episode, I felt a hand on my shoulder as my eyes peeled open.

"Getcho ass up," Collin tapped my shoulder again as I yawned and snickered. "Look," Collin couldn't wait for me to stand before he pointed over to the finished product. "You can getta toddler bed and twin outta dis—"

"I know—Issa convertible bed," I repeated the name of the bed as Collin's face dropped.

"Aw yeah," he laughed with me. "But look—You just grip dis part, lift it up then let it go," he showed me how to lower the rail which I'd need to get baby girl in and out the bed.

"Dats wussup," was all I could say as I eyed the mattress inside.

All that was left to do was decorate my baby girl's bed with the frilly pink shit I bought, last week with my mama. Unbeknownst to Amani, my mama has been on my side when it came to the sex of the baby. We just had this feeling Amani didn't feel. She swore up and down that we were having a boy and even got my daddy and Cairo on her side, since the family was mainly all boys. Outside of the women we chose and married... Banks men have reigned supreme. Up until now. And I was ready for the change my baby girl would make on my family and me. Soften these hard ass niggas up.

Buzzz!

Gripping the right side of my shorts, I didn't even realize I had my phone. After I put Amani back to sleep, I stayed in bed, fighting with sleep, too. I must've grabbed my phone just as I pulled my shorts up. No shirt, just slides, shorts, and a phone.

Buzzz!

"Yeah?" I spoke into the receiver as I looked back at Collin admiring his work.

The sounds of sniffling had me standing straight up as Collin caught sight of my posture and turned to see what was wrong.

"Ma, you a'ight?" I asked, now getting Collin's full attention as he quickly came over to the rocking chair where I was once lounging.

"She's gone..." Was all she could get out before breaking all the way down as my jaw clenched with my fists.

"What?"

I could see the worry in Collin's eyes as he moved closer to me. I didn't even have to tell him before his face cracked, and his head dropped.

BOOM!

Looking up towards the door, my heartbeat started racing as I heard another loud thud. Dropping my phone, I ran towards the noise, knowing something happened to Mani. Tripping as Amani came through before I exited, I didn't want to run into her so I stumbled off to the side.

"Carter!" Amani shrieked holding onto her stomach.

Chest heaving up and down, she waved me over to her but I couldn't move. Her face was flushed as her wide eyes screamed for help. Waving more frantically, I snapped out of whatever space I was in and ran to her side.

"My water just broke!" she burst into tears, shaking her head in disbelief. "I'm too early!" she clawed at my side, gripping my shirt to pull me into her as her eyes closed tightly. "Sss—Ooo, I can't have the baby!"

A contraction must've hit because after a couple seconds she released my shirt and opened her eyes. Still a little shaken, she never took her eyes off me. Like a deer in headlights, I didn't know what to do. I was barely legal when Cairo came into this world and I wasn't even there when Dede's water broke. I came right after she had him and I hated thinking back on that day because of all the bullshit that transpired immediately after my son's birth.

"Carter!" Amani snapped, bringing my focus back to her and out of my head. "We should go to the hospital—*Right?*" She was nodding so my head bobbed up and down too.

That sounded right. *I don't know?* Nodding as I looked over at my brother, he was doing the same shit too.
"TAKE ME!"

CHAPTER NINE

Amani

Carter rolled through the emergency driveway like a bat out of hell. Knocking over a cone set in place to keep cars from parking or driving near the ambulance truck, I cut my eyes over at him because he needed to calm down. Although these contractions were painful, his driving and rushing did more harm than good. Barely putting the truck in park, Carter jumped out and the back door where Collin was sitting opened. He was right behind his brother, taking over the wheel as Carter went to the back to retrieve the diaper bag.

"I'ma park yo shit, Bro and call mama," Collin told Carter who's eyes were on me but he still nodded his head.

I'd packed the hospital bag weeks ago like a few of the baby books had suggested, picking out unisex outfits and blankets to satisfy me and Carter once the baby was born and we knew the sex. He thought he was slick by going behind my back and switching out the baby clothes, but two nights ago, while he was out, I changed them back to the original things I had picked out and hid the bag under the bed and didn't tell him until tonight.

"C'mon baby," Carter had the bag slung over one shoulder so he could help me step out his truck.

Breathing in my nose and out my mouth, none of this crap seemed to be working. The contractions hit, and they were even more painful than the last. I should sue!

"You a'ight?" Carter asked me as we stepped into the hospital.

"Yeah," I nodded my head, just relieved that my contraction had passed.

The nursing staff was already on high alert with the way we pulled into their parking lot so I didn't even have to explain why we came. Carter just gave my name and birthday and they had bracelets on both our arms in less than two minutes. Five minutes in and I got a wheelchair and another minute later Carter was handed a clipboard with paperwork he had to fill out. Something he'd have to put on the back burner because two nurses were already wheeling me out the lobby and towards the elevators.

Blinking and breathing, reality was starting to set in. My baby was on his way and I don't think I'm ready. How can I be? There were so many things I didn't know how to do. I've never really changed a diaper, Carter and I've been to all my prenatal classes but a doll and a baby are so far on the spectrum, it's cute to pretend but I was having a real baby. All the what ifs I shouldn't have been thinking flooded my mind. At the forefront was the idea of me failing as a mother. What if my child grew to hate me or despise some of the things I did like I had with Jewel... And even Julian? They were my parents and I could very well be a hateful witch or a neglectful mother. I could be a pushover when I wanted to be, and I didn't want to give into bad habits. *Oh, my gosh!* I'm really not ready!

"You ready mama?" One of the nurses was all smiles because she didn't know I'd cracked the tip of the iceberg called crazy. "Do you know the gender?" She asked another question, and this time I shook my head. "What are y'all hopin' for?" She asked me and I immediately looked to Carter because I'd forgotten what I wanted or how to speak.

"A beautiful baby girl—Just like her mama," Carter spoke up as he reached for my hand.

Probably knowing how frantic I was, I loved him more, in this moment. Feeling another rip from my roota-to-my-toota, I squeezed his hand and braved it out. Glad that my thoughts ceased during the pain. *I guess that's the best part about all of this.*

"Okay, Mr. Banks," one of the nurses called out to Carter as he glanced in her direction. "This isn't your wife's room... We weren't expecting her so soon but we can check her and the baby's vitals and monitor her while her room is being prepared," she told Carter as he nodded his head up and down. "Sounds good?"

"Yeah dats fine."

"Cool—Amani," the nurse leaned down to get closer to my face as I winced away the pain. "I can tell your contractions are close and that's a great sign," she told me while rubbing my back as I nodded my head, breathing with the pain. "I need you to slip into this gown for me—" Shaking my head, the nurse stopped talking.

I didn't want her touching me, breathing in my space, or

asking me to stand up. I definitely didn't want to change into a gown. I bet walking added to the pain, and I wasn't going. *Nope, not today, not ever!* "It's an easy slip on—"

"No!"

"I'll help her," Carter chimed in as I glared in his direction.

Laughing as the nurses exited, he crouched down beside me with the biggest, goofiest smile plastered to his face.

"I see you gon' be mean as hell in labor," he was tickled pink and all I could see was red as another contraction hit.

How my contractions were coming back-to-back, I don't even know. It hadn't even been a full two hours since my water broke and I was feeling too much pain. And I've read that every labor is different but should it hurt this badly so suddenly?

Helping me out of my shirt, Carter slid the gown over my head and helped me pull it down. Doing most of the work, Carter bore with me as two contractions hit, stopping him from taking my pants off. One leg at a time, he had managed to get my pants off and lift me up so I could limp to the bed.

"You okay?" He asked me as I nodded my head up and down.

And I was telling the truth because I didn't think I'd feel any better until after the baby was born... So I had to suck it up and take it.

Knock. Knock.

"Good, you're ready!" the giddy nurse was back in the room to annoy me. "I'm Jill, this is Aria, we're going to be with you primarily through the birth of your baby—Right now..." Jill moved to the back room cabinets and opened them. "We need to get you hooked on the heart monitors so we can track the heartbeat," she told me as I nodded my head.

Watching her pull out this velcro belt, Jill and Aria lifted me up and stretched the belt as far as it would go before wrapping it tightly around my belly. Feeling like my circulation was being cut off, I struggled to breathe a little.

"It's a little too tight," I told them as Carter scooted closer to me with a scowl on his face.

"I know it's gonna feel tight but we won't be able to get a read on the heartbeat—"

"If it's hurtin' hurt, won't it do more harm than good?" Carter interjected as Jill giggled and shook her head.

"Your wife and the baby are fine, I promise you," she told Carter as she went over to the heart reading machine to cut in on.

Within minutes the low pounding of my baby's heart filled the room. Though I've heard it before, hearing it again made me a little emotional.

"Alright, now we gotta do a cervix test—"

"Can I get an epidural?" I interjected, not caring about anything other than getting rid of this pain.

"We're about to find out, now," Jill told me as I winced from another contraction passing. "How far apart are your contractions?" She asked me as she snapped her blue gloves on, pushing my left leg up then my right.

"I think five minutes..." I looked to Carter for reassurance as he shrugged and nodded.

Bracing myself, I heard the horrors of the cervix test, Both my sisters told me it was the worst. Closing my eyes as she got down and between my legs, it took only a second for me to find out just how bad this test was.

"AHHH!" I screeched, as Carter grabbed my hand.

Still frowning, he knew there was nothing he could do to help. She was digging—Clawing, is what it felt like and I didn't know what she was supposed to find but I wanted her to stop soon after she began.

"It's—Just a little more," Jill told me as she twisted and poked and screwed my insides.

I hate this bitch!

"Okay..." her voice was uncertain as she finally pulled her hand out of me to stand up. "I don't know..." She paused to breathe as her coworker came to her, pulling Jill aside.

Already worrying, I looked to Carter, pleading with my eyes. His jaw clenched as he watched the two nurses intently before I squeezed his hand to get his attention.

"Wuss goin' on?" He asked after peaking down at me.

"Her water is broken," Jill started out like I hadn't been there when it happened. "And usually, that's a sign to push—But you're only three centimeters dilated," she dropped her shoulders as my mind when back to a few inserts from the baby book I read. "Not only that..." she turned to look over her shoulder at Aria. "The baby's breech and it's an easy fix but considering how small the opening is—It's gonna be painful," Jill spoke as another contraction hit.

"I don't wanna do this, Carter," I cried out to Carter because all the news I was getting was bad.

That's a sign, right? I wasn't cut out to be a mother, and this just confirms it.

"No, no, no—*Shhh*," Jill came to my side. "I'm only telling you this out of obligation to inform but not alarm. The baby's fine but we have to turn *him*—"

"*Her*," Carter quickly corrected Jill as her eyes rounded.

"Oh, I was under the impression that y'all haven't found out—"

"Issa girl—"

"Carter!" I winced, not wanting to hear another peep about this girl or boy situation while I was contracting and trying to flip this baby around.

BEEP. BEEP. BEEP. BEEP. BEEP. BEEP.

Like clockwork, the heart monitor beeped, silencing the voices and garnering everyone's attention. My anxiety was through the roof as I watched the printing papers with overdrawn scribbles pour from the machine. I had no clue what they meant, but I assumed it wasn't good.

"Okay, this isn't good—"

"What?" Carter and I both asked.

"Just a second—"

"No! You just said my baby was fin—"

"*She* is," Jill nodded frantically as she ran out the room.

"Go get her—"

"No, that's not a good idea," Aria spoke up as Carter released my hand. "She's coming back—"

"Why she leave in da first place—Y'all unprofessional as fuck!" Carter snapped as I breathed through another contraction as a knot formed in my belly, producing a pain more severe than the last contraction.

Knocking the wind from my lungs as I sat up to clutch the hardened part of my belly, Jill had it right. Something was wrong, and nobody was telling me.

"Just lie back—"

"I CAN'T!" I yelled at Aria just as Jill came back through the door, this time with a team of men and women. "WHAT—"

"We need to prep her for emergency surgery—"

"Surgery?" Carter repeated as Jill tossed a blue packet at his chest.

"Your wife has to deliver cesarian, right now—Put those scrubs on *dad*, and let's get moving!"

Watching Carter rip the blue package open, he was characteristically calm, but I saw the look in his eyes. He could no longer mask his emotions with me but knowing he was trying only scared me even more. My eyes were raining rivers over the thought of my body not being able to deliver vaginally. What was so wrong with my canal that I needed to be cut open? Okay, so the baby was breeched... Well, turn *him* around! That's an easy fix.

"Can't we just wait—"

"You're not fully dilated and the longer you wait the higher your risks of—"

"*AIN'T SHIT HAPPENIN' TO MY BABY!*" Carter and I both blurted out to the pushy nurse who hadn't stopped talking and explaining since we came in.

The side of my lip curled at how in sync Carter, and I was at this very moment. Not normally a vulgar person, I'd be damned if this bitch or anybody, for that matter, spoke ill over my unborn. I'd managed to move, become acclimated with a new city and state, go to school—Graduate and carry this baby almost to term... I was going to have my baby the way I planned. Straight out my hoo-ha and so help me, GOD—*Him! That's who should be fixing this!*

I've heard Carter's prayers before bed and in the shower when he thought he was alone. He even prayed faithfully over his food so this shouldn't be happening to me.

"As much as you prayed this should be a cakewalk," I spat over at Carter as he exhaled and shook his head.

"You not finna blame God for dis—"

"Why not?" My bottom lip trembled as Carter clenched his jaw. "I should be able to have my baby like everybody else—"

"You not everybody else!" Carter talked over me as I shuddered from the amount of stress my tears were putting me under. "Listen to me," Carter crouched down so that our eyes leveled.

Cupping my chin into his palm, I swallowed and gazed into

his emerald-like orbs. *I hope the baby inherits those*, I told myself as I waited for him to speak.

"You carried *her* as long as you could—*Shhh...*" Carter calmly shushed me as I nodded my head. "*She's* fine, okay?" I could see his eyes misting and that didn't help my current state but by the tone of his voice and how sure he seemed, a strange calmness rolled over me as I nodded my head confidently. "We finna go in da O.R.—I'ma be right beside you," Carter told me as I continued nodding as he spoke off the plan. "See, look at me," he stood up quickly to show off his blue scrubs. "I'm scrubbed up—Ready for whatever," Carter squatted back down, gripping my chin again. "We finna go in there, together, and comes back out wit a healthy, beautiful baby girl, a'ight?" He placed his forehead to mine as my vision clouded with tears. "*A'ight?*"

"Okay," I blinked out a few tears as Carter lifted his head up to kiss the spot his head touched.

"Okay, what?"

"Okay, let's do it—"

"You gon' gimme a lil girl?" he asked as I smiled and nodded. "See..." Carter balled his left hand into a fist to commemorate this moment.

Finally, after months of opposing arguments, I'd come to his side. It didn't even matter if we were both wrong... After the pep talk my husband had just given me, I'd work tirelessly through the years to give him his little girl.

"Are we ready?" Jill was wearing a soft smile as I exhaled and nodded my head up and down.

"*We're* ready," I confirmed, reaching for Carter's hand.
It's time!

CHAPTER TEN

Carter

Rubbing my hands together as I watched the anesthesiologist sedate my wife she slowly began to relax, reaching for my hand again. Taking it into mine, I squeezed it to get her to look over at me. Winking, I mouthed for her to relax and watched her nod and exhale, dropping her shoulders in the process. Holding onto her hand as I eyed the Doctor walking behind the curtain, I wanted to be on the other side but I didn't want Amani to freak out. Blowing air into my cheeks and keeping it there, I counted and waited and counted and inhaled and exhaled, constantly looking down at Amani to make sure she wasn't anxious, in pain, or just stressed out.

She looked fine. A couple minutes under anesthesia will probably do that to you. Smirking as the droopy look on her face curled into a smile, I knew Shawty was gone. Faded as fuck.

"Why are you smiling?" she asked as I showed a little more of my teeth.

"Cuz you gone, *huh*?" I laughed with her, watching Amani lift her shoulders.

"Mama's okay?" one of the nurses asked me and Amani as I nodded my head.

"She good—You a'ight, baby?" I spoke directly to Amani as she nodded and smiled brighter for me. "See, dat smile—"

"Gorgeous!" the same nurse complimented Amani as she blushed up at me. "We're almost finished, *Papa*!" she was now speaking to me as my anxiety rose.

Rocking from left to right, I was shifting my weight to each leg since I couldn't pace the Operating room. Growing more anxious as the surgeon called out instructions and requests, the worst being the scalpel he would use to incise my wife. Swallowing, knowing she couldn't feel a thing, hearing those words—

"First incision..."

Had me gripping my stomach, tensing and wincing. Keeping my eyes on everybody else behind the curtain, I'd neglected to see about Amani. She hadn't squeezed my hand or made much noise since sedation and I guess that was a good thing. They had an oxygen mask covering her lips and nose so I knew she could breathe and her heart monitor was steady.

"Clamps!"

Breathing out, every time the surgeon spoke, I could feel my baby girl itching to get out. We were so near to her birth I didn't know if I could take any more of the suspense. Everything was so calm and quiet, outside of the machine noises and the clanking of used medical utensils as they hit the sanitation bowls, I couldn't stop my anxiety from rising. Usually, I knew how to conduct my emotions. Keeping them at bay but these last couple weeks have revealed a person I wasn't too familiar with. Amani could pick up on mood swings and emotional rifts like a hawk and she was almost always the person who would redirect negative attitudes or calm me down. I wasn't used to having anybody so close that they could read me so well, yet here she was. The chaos I kept hidden from the rest of the world was her playground. To regroup, rearrange, and redirect...

Feeling a weak squeeze, I looked down to see Amani gazing up at me. I couldn't see her mouth but her eyes were smiling, trying to ease my current chaotic state. *See, what I mean?* It's like she felt this shit with me. Giving her a phony smile, she squeezed my hand again causing me to laugh. *She knew I was forcing it.* This time, the smile was genuine.

"Alright, I'm pulling the baby out," I heard the doctor say. "Almost—"

WAHHH!

Looking up from Amani as cries filled the room, and my heart skipped a beat. Letting Amani's hand go, my blood was rushing to my head as the room got hot and started spinning. Swallowing the spit in my mouth, I blinked a couple times because I couldn't believe she was here.

"Daddy, you wanna give us a hand?" Jill called out to me as I blinked twice before nodding my head.

Swiping my hand down my face, I looked to Amani, this time for reassurance as she gracefully smirked and nodded her head. Taking a deep breath, I nodded back and started making my way to the other side of the curtain. *There goes my baby!* I gushed as the biggest smile spread across my face. Covered in blood and fluids, my baby girl—*I knew it!*

"You were right, *Papa*—Here's your little girl!" The nurse gently placed her into my arms, and her cries ceased.

Blinking away tears as I looked into her chinky, glossy green eyes a silly smile covered the lower half of my face. My baby was a doll. I couldn't stop staring as she wiggled slightly in my hands.

"You gotta support the neck, like this," one of the nurses maneuvered my fingers until my baby girl stopped moving. "See, there ya go—You wanna put her on mama?" she suggested as I looked to the curtain, completely forgetting Amani behind there.

Nodding my head without taking my eyes off my baby, I could hear a few of the medical staff laughing at me but I didn't care. I had my baby girl... Finally.

"Let's cut the cord," the same nurse who'd help me hold my baby lifted her out of my hands as my face cracked. "I'm gonna give her back," she promised just as my baby started wailing at the top of her lungs. "Oh, boy... You're a daddy's girl already!" The nurse giggled with her colleagues as another one handed me the sheers. "Right between the clamps—*Yup*... Awesome!"

Watching as a team of nurses with blankets wiped and diapered baby girl, they swaddled her just as quickly and placed this screaming little girl back in my arms. Ceasing the tears as I lifted her to my face, I was proud. Kissing her red cheeks, I slowly made the walk back behind the curtain where Amani was waiting patiently. Gently placing baby girl onto Amani, she rubbed her cheek to Amani's as I smiled looking on proudly. *My baby really just had my baby!*

"I was right," I told Amani as she rolled her eyes.

CHAPTER ELEVEN

Amani

Propped up against my pillows, Carter was taking extra precaution in my healing process. I had my bandage changed daily, pillows fluffed and reissued when he felt they weren't soft or fluffy enough. Soups and crackers he brought in from Panera and even a 32-ounce Speedway cup filled with ice so I could suck and chew and be content. My second day into recovery, I was told me and the baby would be discharged tomorrow evening and I couldn't wait. My patience was wearing thin. I couldn't pee in peace, couldn't eat or sleep or just have me time. There was always somebody coming and going and I was over it.

"Put her down," I urged Carter fearing Chandler would become attached and crave to be held from here on out. "You're gonna spoil her—"

"And so what," Carter pecked the top of her head as he rocked back and forth in his seat. "I'ma be da one holdin' her."

Of course that would be his response. Sighing as I scooped another spoonful of soup, I could hear Carter mocking my sigh with a longer one. Smirking but keeping my eyes on my soup, I wasn't about to play with him today.

"SURPRISE!" Ebony's voice filled the room as I glanced over towards the door at her million and one pink, foil balloons and giggled. "We would've came yesterday but Carter told us about your C-section and my mama suggested we give you a full day to recover—"

"And blow up those balloons, *huh?*" I quipped as Collin laughed agreeing with me.

"I told Eb not to do dis shit," Collin smacked his lips as he came over to where his brother was sitting.

Bending down with a smile on his face, he stuck his finger into Chandler's hand, grinning once she gripped it tightly. Watching the three of them coo over her put a smile on my face as my heart fluttered. These Banks men had tough exteriors, but they were only to shield all that mush they carried on the inside.

"*Eh*, look," Carter tapped Collin as he pulled the hat from Chandler's head.

"She a ginger?" Collin laughed in shock. "Just like Granny D!" He was in awe as my hands clutched my chest.

"And she came a few hours after Granny passed—"

"Granny D died?" I was ear hustling hard as Carter and Collin looked my way. "You didn't tell me—"

"Cuz you was in labor—"

"But you could've told me," I could feel my eyes misting as Carter and Collin took a deep breath.

"Mani..." Carter's voice was stern and low as he handed Chandler to her uncle so he could come to my side. "You know you would've been a wreck after allat shit we went through just to bring *Dot* into dis world... You ain't need da added stress of Granny passing," he told me but I didn't hear anything after *Dot*.

"Dot?" I repeated as he smirked and nodded.

"I figure since Chandler look like Granny D then we should nickname her *Dot*—"

"It's *befitting*," Collin added as the room rumbled with laughter.

"Befitting my *ass*," I rolled my eyes as Collin's bottom lip hung open.

"Bro gotcho ass out here cussin'—Damn..." Collin shook his head disapprovingly. "Don't worry, Dot, I'ma be here to make sure you have a normal life—"

"Shut up!" Me and Carter giggled.

"Where mama at—"

"Good morning!" Mr. Banks was all smiles as he came through the door with Cairo racing right behind him.

"Hey, Mani!" Cairo jumped up to the edge of my bed as Carter lurched forward to block him from jumping on me.

"Eh, chill out, Ro—You can't jump on Mani cuz she got stitches," he explained to his son as Cairo's eyes widened with fascination.

"You got stitches?" He asked as I nodded my head. "Why?"

"Your little sister had to be delivered through cesarian," I told him as he scrunched up his face in confusion.

"Is dat like a C-section?" He asked another question as I smiled and nodded my head. "Wow..." Cairo looked and sounded like his father garnering a couple laughs from everybody in the room. "Wuss her name?"

"Chandler," I beamed as Cairo's face curled even more.

"*Chandler?*" He got Collin and his father laughing with that one.

"It's a name I like—"

"Nah, it's a boy's name from a whack ass TV show," Carter interjected as I cut my eyes over at him.

"Ten season isn't what I would call whack—"

"She talkin' bout Friends?" Collin lifted his eyes from Chandler as Carter smacked his lips nodding. "No, you didn't lil sis—I know you ain't mark my niece wit dis name cuz of dat show..." he shook his head as he looked back down at Chandler.

"I don't care what y'all say, I still love Friends," I told them crossing my arms over my chest as Carter scoffed. "And there's nothing you can do because we already signed the papers—"

"I thought Carter was pickin' her name since he was right?" Collin tossed in something Carter wouldn't stop telling me since our daughter was born.

"Stop looking at me," I told Carter as his left brow rose in my direction. "We came to an agreement that I could name her since I went through a lot—"

"Nah... You copped out, bro," Collin was egging Carter on.

"*Lin,* cut it out," Ebony spoke up before I could.

"Say, man, I'm just sayin'..." he smacked him lips. "It couldn't be me—"

"Oh it will!" Ebony heard his mumblings as the both of them shared a laugh.

"Y'all finna..." Carter chimed in as his little brother and his girlfriend scrunched up their faces while shaking their heads. "Don't act like it's impossible--Livin' together will prolly speed up da process—"

"Not when you're faithfully taking your birth control," Ebony added with her finger raised as she pursed her lips together matter-of-factly.

"Yeah, a'ight," Carter was still on the opposing side but he couldn't argue with Ebony's proven method.

She hadn't gotten pregnant yet, and it was going on a year of her and Collin living under the same roof. As right as Carter can be, I think he might be wrong on this one. *I might have to ask her the name of whatever she was taking.* Because I'll be doggoned if Carter puts eighteen months between these babies. Two years max!

"Where mama at?" Carter asked his father as his phone started buzzing. "I was just askin' bout you," he smiled into his screen before turning it on me.

"Hi, Mama!" ksks gushed the second she saw me. "You look so beautiful—"

"Glowing!" I heard a voice I wasn't too familiar with until the phone shifted, revealing Mama Bank's sister, Rachel. "Hi, Mani!" She smiled, and I mirrored her expression. "How ya feelin'?"

"Better," I sighed, just glad it was all over. "How are y'all holding up?" My mind was off the birth of my daughter, and onto Granny D's sudden passing.

"It doesn't feel real," Mama Megan spoke up as I nodded my head understandingly. "And I've had months to process this but…" She exhaled and I could see her face drop as she swallowed back tears. "We're gonna get through this…" Her voice was heavy as I lowered my eyes to my hands. "But, um—She did say something interesting before she left," Mama Megan's face lit up as I looked back at the screen.

"She told us that baby's on her way!" Rachel couldn't wait so she blurted it out before her big sister could.

"Yeah—I was just tellin' Collin how crazy it was dat *Dot* came a couple hours after Granny left," Carter chuckled softly.

"*Dot?*" Mama Megan and her sister said together.

"Yeah—Hol'up," Carter motioned for Collin to come to his side. "She look just like Granny, mama—Pale, rosy, and red," Carter laughed as he put the camera on Chandler's face.

"Oh, my goodness!" I could hear the tears in Mama Megan's voice as I teared up. "She's mama all over again!" she gushed as I giggled and sobbed. "Y'all named her *Dorothy?*"

"Hell nah—Mani named her *Chandler*," Carter scoffed as his daddy and Collin chuckled.

"I *love* that name!" Rachel beamed as I smugly looked over at Carter who was smacking his lips and shaking his head. "Just like Friends—"

"Yes! Chandler Bing!" I was happy someone else, other than myself, could partake in my favorite show.

"Rachel Green has her Chandler Bing!" Rachel laughed with me as everybody in the room, with me, looked on with screw faces.

"Dats da white side I'm afraid of comin' out of me," Collin shook his head as Carter, Ebony, and Mr. Banks laughed.

"*Nigga!*" Carter chimed in, shaking up with his brother. "Cuz I refuse!"

"I thought y'all weren't ashamed of your white side," Ebony teased as brothers smacked their lips, waving her off.

"We ain't," they spoke in unison.

"But I can't be like dat," Collin pointed to me and his brother's phone as I gasped

"Well, I'm offended—"

"You ain't no offended," Carter called my bluff as the room erupted in laughter. "Yo ass just lame, like I been tellin' you—"

"Am not!"

"*Am not!*" Carter and Collin mocked me as we laughed again.

"Shut up—"

"Y'all leave her alone," Mama Megan and her sister came to my defense as I stuck my tongue out at Collin and Carter.

"You got in trouble!" I added fuel to the fire.

"*Knock, knock!*"

Looking to the door, I almost leaped from my bed as both my sisters came through the door. Carter help onto my shoulder as I wiggled in my bed for them to come closer.

"Is this her?" Fatima couldn't wait to get to Chandler. "Oh my goodness—Hi, beautiful!" she gushed as she sniffed the top of the baby's head. "I love the smell of babies!"

"We know," Salimah jabbed as she hugged me. "Y'all gotta whole starting five!"

"Shut up," Fatima playfully rolled her eyes as she made her way to me with Chandler in her arms. "How was it?"

"Painful—"

"Oh, don't we know it," Salimah exhaled. "But it's worth it—"

"I had to have a C-section," I admitted to my sisters ashamed.

"So—The baby's here, healthy, and beautiful so you did good, mommy," Salimah kissed my cheek before she took Chandler from Fatima.

"Hey!" Fatima protested as Salimah quickly turned her back to her.

"Wait, lemme see her!"

It was like being kids all over again. Salimah wouldn't even give Fatima a full minute of something she wanted too. Shaking my head as I watched them sniff and rub her hair, I couldn't help but smile. The love was overwhelming in a good way.

"Where's Ty—"

"Right here—Wussup, Mani!" Tyrone came in the room, shaking up with Collin, Carter, and their father before pulling Ebony into a hug. "How you doin'?" he asked as he leaned in to hug me, too.

"Better," I giggled.

"Damn, Carter knew all along," Tyrone chuckled as he peered over his wife's shoulder to look at Chandler. "Wuss her name?"

"*Chandler!*" Carter, Ebony, Collin, Mr. Banks, Mrs. Banks and her sister, still on the phone, answered him.

"Damn—Why everybody so strong wit it?" Tyrone chuckled with us.

"I love it!" Fatima told me as I grinned. "It's so her—"

"It ain't no *so her...*" Collin smacked his lips getting the men in the room to laugh.

"Yeah it is—It's different, and it has a ring to it—"

"What ring?" Collin asked as Fatima exhaled causing him to laugh.

"Her name sounds like one of those 90210, Beverly Hills names—You know when they grow up privileged, and wealthy..." Fatima was right as my eyes widened at her words. "Like you can see her name in the tabloids—*Chandler Banks does it again!*" Fatima used her hands, placing one on her hip and the other in the air to strike a pose as we all laughed. "See, y'all know what I mean!"

"It does sound like that," I told my baby sister as Salimah giggled and nodded.

"And she will!" Mama Megan added, reminding me that she and her sister were still on the phone.

"Just like a grandma to buy into everything," Collin laughed with his brother. "*My grandbaby gon' be rich and famous, you watch!*" his voice was higher as his impression of his mother sent everybody into laughter.

"Wussup," Torin's voice picked up as he shook up with Carter, their father, then Collin. "Mani," he nodded towards me as I grinned, doing the same. "Congratulations."

"Thank you."

Our relationship had changed significantly before the family trip to Dubai. We weren't extremely close, but we had a better understanding of each other. And he wasn't as mean or rude as he had been before.

"What took you so long?" Fatima asked him as he looked towards the door, getting everybody to do the same.

The hospital staff were piled outside of my room, grinning as they tried to look busy. *Oh my God*, I exhaled already knowing why they were pining around.

"*Ohhh*," Collin caught on too. "You already know they finna blow da magazines up—"

"Eh, close da door," Carter called out as Tyrone hopped to do it. "Shit—Dats da last thing we need—"

"Don't worry bout it—I got security wit me," Torin assured my husband. "I'll leave some here when we leave too, so y'all can get out without too much fuss."

"Already," Carter shook up with Torin again.

"Wuss da baby—"

"*Chandler!*" This time, everybody but Torin, spoke up as we all laughed.

"Ya'll gon' leave my baby's name alone!" I rolled my eyes as Carter leaned down to kiss the side of my face.

With everybody holding their own conversations and hovering over Chandler, Carter and I had a moment for ourselves. Staring into his eyes, I could hear his words. *Thank you*. Grinning as I cocked my head to the side, I winked, *you're welcome*. Showing me his teeth, *I love you*, he bowed his head forward as I blushed, miring his expression. Always beating me to those three words. *I love you more;* I bit down on my bottom lip before poking them back out so Carter could peck them. *What's understood doesn't have to be explained—Or spoken, in our case.*

CHAPTER TWELVE

Carter

"A'ight, lil mama—Whatchu want?" I asked Dot as the entire house filled with the sounds coming from his tiny mouth.

Since two, this morning, she's been crying and my eyes were bloodshot red, trying to quiet her down enough so everybody could sleep. Since she'd been born, I could just hold her, and she was content but I guess after a week daddy lost his touch. Shit kind of hurt, too. Dot was supposed to be my baby, but she was showing out for her mama.

"Here," Amani motioned for me to hand Dot off to her and as much as I didn't want to... I did.

Reluctantly placing my baby girl into her mama's arms, her screams grew as I giddily took her back. Smiling smugly, Amani groaned loud enough for me to know she wasn't in the mood. Kissing the top of Chandler's sweaty head, she was red all over and I didn't like the sight of it. My mama used to say nothing good came from a crying baby—Especially as long as Chandler had been going at it. Almost thirty minutes and we still didn't know what she wanted.

Amani tried feeding, burping, checking her diaper, to which we just went ahead and changed to see if it would make a difference. *It didn't.* She wasn't old enough to be teething, but I massaged her gums, anyway. And she momentarily sucked on my fingers for a second, then went back to crying. Another five minutes of this shit and I would be forced to call in the big guns... Meagan Arlene Banks.

"UGHHH—What does she want?" Amani moved her hands as she spoke, letting me know she was on the brink of a meltdown.

Hell, nah, I told myself as I shook my head. I wasn't about to have a house full of crazy ladies giving me hell. Exhaling, I kissed Chandler's forehead again, then it hit me. *I know what to do!* Bopping my head to the beat in my head, I swayed around with Chandler tucked in the crook of my left arm like a football so I could snap my right hand fingers. Catching the glare from Amani each time I spun around and could see her face.

"Carter, please don't do this—"

"*I've been thinkin' bout you, for quite a while. You're on my mind every day and every night—My every thought is you... The things you do-ooo! Seems so satisfying to me, I must confess it girl—*"

To my surprise and Amani's dismay, my voice was the key —*I got my magic back!* Chandler's eyes were wide in wonder as I continued serenading her. Dancing in the middle of my bedroom with Amani perched, agitated with me on the edge of the bed.

"*Ooo, and I like it! You send chills up my spine, every time I take one look at you. Girl you're blowing my mind with the things you say to me...*" Shimmying up to Amani as the left corner of her mouth twitched until she was grinning and rolling her eyes.

Reaching for her hand, she crossed both arms over her chest defiantly, looking off to the side as I stepped closer to her. Cupping her chin and moving her face so she would look my way, her grin had stretched to reveal her teeth. Nodding for her to give into me, Amani's shoulders dropped as her arms fell to her side. Sighing with another roll of her eyes, she took my hand, and I pulled her up immediately. Into me, I released her hand, wrapping my arm around her waist as all three of us rocked around the room, now. Gazing into Amani's bright brown eyes, I wanted her to feel the bridge was written by me for her.

"*Girl lemme run this by you—Just one more time. You're on my mind every day and every night. My every thought is you, the things you do. Seems so satisfying to me—I must confess it girl—*"

"*OOO, AND I LIKE IT!*" Cairo stepped through the door, on cue.

Giggling, Amani looked back at my son who'd joined me in putting a smile on the girls' faces. Letting go of Amani, I lifted Chandler into the air as I spun us around slowly, careful enough so her head was supported and she didn't get too dizzy.

"*I like the way you comb ya hair. And I like those stylish clothes you wear—It's just the little things you do. That show how much you really care—Like when I fell in love with you just watchin' ya mama give birth to you... Yoooou gave me another reason to live!*" I had to change some words for my baby girl as she watched me intently.

My mama was right... This girl was too smart. Alert, already and she ain't even been here a good week and a half. Two-stepping back over to her mama, I pulled Amani back into my arms and grooved around the room with her, still singing.

"*I like it. I like it—I really really like it. I'm for it, adore it, so come let me enjoy it...*" Cairo help me with the ending chorus.

"*I like it-Uh-That's right—Uh-huh, I like it, yeah—Muah!*" I leaned into Amani and pecked her lips as her chest caved and she melted all over me and Chandler. "*Daddy* still got it—*Huh*, Chandler?"

Amani's face was redder than Dot's when we finished. Giggling as I showered her with kisses, I could hear Cairo making gagging noises but I ain't care. He ain't get it now but a couple years from now he'd understand what I felt—Hopefully, not until he hit his late teens. Because I ain't tryna bring no grandkids into this world before his high school graduation.

"What I tell you before you delivered, Dot?" I asked Amani as she grinned and bowed her head. "Nah, don't do dat—" I lifted Amani's head using her chin as she grinned before tucking her bottom lip into her mouth. "Daddy not finna leave you witta baby."

"*Oh,* you my daddy, now?" Amani cooed as I nodded my head confidently.

"Been dat nigga—"

"Stop it," she melted into my arms before looking over her shoulder to see Cairo's eyes wide and rim as he looked on.

"Mind ya bidness—Take ya sister and go watch somethin' on Netflix," I held Dot up for Cairo as Amani quickly shook her head.

"No, Cai, he's just playing—Carter, cut it out!" She giggled with me. "But thank you both for being the best daddy and big brother ever," Amani told us as she pulled Cairo into a hug.

Running her finger through his waves, like she would with

my hair before kissing the top of his forehead. Smiling up at her, nothing made me happier than seeing Amani love on my son like she carried and had him. And I knew Cairo loved her because she was all he talked about. Always wanting to get her gifts, cookies, and little shit she enjoyed just to put a smile on her face.

Pecking Amani lips before I turned her loose, I realized Hulu had the latest episode of Good Doctor waiting on me. Heading out the room with Cairo, he looked up smiling. Ruffling my hand through his hair as we made it to his room, Cairo was eager to get back on his game.

"Nah, it's late—You can play in da mornin'," I told his as he exhaled sharply then nodded. "Goodnight—"

"Night, dad," he was salty but so what.

Taking my baby girl to her room, she was snoring softly, just like her mama. Mouth ajar and red on the nose from all the crying she'd just took the whole house through. Kissing her nose as she jolted in her sleep, I chuckled when she didn't open her eyes. Baby girl done wore herself out. Carefully placing her in her crib, I felt a finger swipe across my back as I looked over my shoulder to see Amani grinning and hugging me from behind. Leaving the crib gate down, Dot was still too young to climb out.

"She put us through it, tonight," Amani sighed as I turned around still in her hold.

"Yeah, I know... But we doin' dis," I assured her as she nodded her head slowly, watching Dot sleep peacefully.

With her chin glued to my chest, I rested my chin on top of her head as we watch Dot some more. Crazy how shit can change so drastically in one year. You don't even think this far ahead even when life comes at you fast. Three hundred and sixty-five days is nothing and yet I still didn't foresee another child and a wife in that timeframe.

"Hey," Amani lifted her head up, knocking it into my chin. "I'm sorry," she winced while reaching for my face to make sure I was okay.

"Yo big head ass always knocking into me," I groaned as she giggled and apologized some more.

"I'm sorry, babe," Amani giggled, now rubbing my chin with both her hands. "Let's go watch Good Doctor!" She suggested as I fought the smile slowly spreading across my face.

"I swear I love you—"

"I know," Amani winked as she walked backwards, taking my hands into hers. "I love you, too," she told me before turning around so I could hug her from behind and walk us back into our bedroom.

"Damn, I can't wait for deez six weeks to be up," I grumbled thinking about how much longer I still had to go.

"Oh my gosh," Amani giggled, choosing to leave it at that.

She better or else I might just say fuck it and see how far we can go tonight. *There's gotta be something we can do to ease this waiting period.*

CHAPTER THIRTEEN

Amani

N‍IBBLING ON MY BOTTOM LIP AS C‍ARTER KEPT HIS EYES on the road, we'd been driving since six this morning, after picking up Cairo. All last night, I was glued to his side because I just felt his playful spirit plummet. In two more hours, all of Mama Megan's family would come together to put their matriarch to rest. After two weeks of putting it off, due to the birth of Chandler, whom everybody else lovingly referred to as Dot because she looked an awful lot like Granny Dorothy. The irony of God to make her entrance into this world after her great-grandmother took her last bow and exited stage left.

Feeling Carter's fingers intertwine with mine, I glanced over as he lifted the back of my hand to his lips, kissing it. One hand on the wheel and the other in mine, Carter never took his eyes off the road. And I know he was only focusing this hard to keep reality from settling. One of his childhood heroes was being laid to rest and I could see the chip forming on his shoulder the closer we got to the funeral home. Looking down at my black dress, I've always hated this about funerals. Even in mourning, why did we have to wear it on our clothes? It only further dampened the mood, leaving no space to remember the better times.

"Ro?" Carter's voice picked up inside my head as I looked to see him peering through the rearview mirror.

"Yes, sir?"

"You awake?"

"*Yeah*—I been up dis whole time," Cairo yawned and stretched.

"You a'ight?" Carter asked his son who nodded in lieu of verbally responding. "Dot still sleep?" He asked, and Cairo nodded again. "*A'ight*—We almost there," Carter swallowed before taking his eyes from the mirror to look over at me. "You a'ight?" he asked me as I nodded.

"Are you okay?"

"Yeah," his jaw twitched as he spoke and I knew he wasn't being honest.

Squeezing his hand, his brows furrowed.

"What?"

"Are you?" I pressed the issue as he sighed and shrugged.

"As a'ight as I'ma be, Shawty," he spoke truthfully as I twisted my lips. "But don't worry about it..." he kissed the back of my hand as he turned into the funeral home parking lot. "I'ma be a'ight—*A'ight*?"

"Okay," I decided to leave the conversation for a later day.

He was right... Today he was going to be sad, cry, and probably be questioning God but in time, he'd come to accept it. I'll just make it my job to make sure he's not stressed out so he can get over the first stages of grief. Letting go of my hand, Carter shut off the engine and opened his door. Going to the back, where Dot's car seat sat, he opened her door, popping the seat from its station. Cairo was out next, grabbing Dot's bag and slinging it over his shoulders as I smiled as I watched him. Since we came home, Cairo has been the best big brother in the world. I couldn't help thinking of all the times I used to wish for a brother like him when I was younger. My daughter had everything I wanted and needed—A daddy who doted over her and a loving big brother who was first to protect her and quick with whatever she needed when she cried. She had uncles waiting to burst hell wide open if anything happened to her... I couldn't be any happier.

"C'mon, mama," Carter told me as he opened my door, holding his hand out so I could step out in these heels.

Seeing him bite down on his lip, I shook my head because Carter was always going to be mannish.

"Remember where we are," I reminded him as he smirked and shook his head.

"I ain't doin' nothing, Shawty—C'mon," he tried to brush it off as we giggled up to the entrance.

Taking my hand into his, Carter led us to the side of the building where most of his family was standing beside. Near the wall, Mama Megan, Mr. Banks, all the sisters, Collin, and Ebony waited. Letting go of my hand to shake up with his daddy, brother, and cousins, I'd only met once, at my baby shower... I hugged Mama Megan, first. Allowing her to squeeze and rock us from side to side as she sniffled and got all her feels out.

"How are ya beautiful?" she asked as she pulled back.

"I'm doing good—How you holding up?"

"I don't know," was all she said as she sniffled, swiping her finger underneath her eyes.

"If you need anything from me and *Dot,* you know I'll drop everything to be there," I told her as she giggled, looking at Carter as he came to my side, still holding Dot's car seat.

"And I might need a full day with my grandbabies," she sniffled as Cairo wrapped his arms around his Grammy. "Hi baby," she kissed the top of his head.

"Don't cry, Grammy," Cairo returned a kiss to her cheek, as he swiped his hand across her cheeks. "You want me to spin-na night?" He asked as Collin laughed first, alerting Carter who joined his brother.

"You know you're always welcomed," Mama Megan squeezed her grandson tighter. "So, I guess that means I'm taking my *Dot,* too?" she was looking at me but the question was aimed at Dot's daddy.

I didn't mind it but Carter would have another episode of separation anxiety and I don't think I was prepared to deal with that after this funeral. Twisting my lips as I peered over at Carter, he was already trying to look in another direction to keep from answering his mama.

"Stop," I slapped the side of his arm as he snickered.

"Whatchu need two babies in yo hotel room for, ma?" Carter grumbled, and I knew to stay out of it.

"You don't get to ask me how I'll fair with two babies—I had three or did you forget!" Mama Megan nudged Carter as he shook his head laughing. "Rachel, you and Collin—And Collin was a crybaby!"

"*Eh*—Dis ain't about me!" Collin interjected as we laughed at him. "You always gettin' some shit started—"

"I ain't say none bout you!" Carter barked back at his brother, trying to muff him without shaking the car seat.

"*Aha*! You missed!" Collin flicked Carter's cheek before darting behind Ebony. "Eb, beat his ass for me!"

"You hell, bro gon' use yo girl as a shield!" Carter and Collin laughed as they continued passing licks like little boys.

Just as Carter finally landed a lick, Dot wailed from underneath her blanket tent. Smacking his lips and snapping back into daddy mode, Collin laughed as Carter held the car seat steady so I could peer inside to look at Dot. Since we'd left the hospital, her color had come in, brown tinted like almond milk, the red hues of her hair complimented her skin tone. Paired with her daddy's eyes, she reminded me of a tanned Raggedy Ann with the freckles and all. She might've gotten maybe two things from me. My nose and my puffy bottom lip. Other than that, she took after Carter's side... Which was to be expected considering how much her big brother favored their father.

"Are you hungry?" I talked to Dot as I dug in her diaper bag Cairo was still carrying. "I got just what you need," I cooed, pulling the four ounce bottle out, popping off the top.

Holding the bottle in her mouth, Mama Megan lifted the blankets over the hood and grabbed her big to outline her neck so she wouldn't ruin her dress. It didn't matter because it was hell getting Dot into it. She hated the stockings, the itchiness of the lining to puff out the dress and the shoes—*Boy, the shoes*. Dot hated covering her feet.

"Aren't you just yummy," Mama Megan cooed as she played with Dot's feet.

Hearing the door creak open, every head turned in its direction. The usher, white-gloved and holding his program motioned for us to come in.

"We're ready for the family," he said as he graciously held the door open for us. "My condolences to the Kramer, Scotts,

Banks, and Mayfields," he hung his head in respect as we all filed through the door.

Reaching for Carter's hand, he happily took mine and led us through the door as I slung my arm over Cairo's shoulder. This was us, a family of four. *All for one and one for all, lol! Don't judge me!*

CHAPTER FOURTEEN

Carter

S%%TANDING BESIDE MY WIFE AND SON WITH D%%OT TUCKED between my arm and chest, I dapped and hugged everybody who came to pay my Granny D her respects. From distant relatives to old colleagues who could barely saw us, everybody ran through the line of Granny D's children, grandchildren, and great-grandchildren. Some of them crying, other laughing because they had something funny to share that my granny had told them, to which I smiled, to keep from crying because although funny, I knew I wouldn't get to share another moment like that with Granny in this life.

The service was beautiful, though. Granny had on her navy blue dress with the sequin. My mama claimed it was her favorite so her sisters rolled with it. I almost lost it when I walked up to view her body, though, because she was wearing the *Dolla* pin me and Collin got her back in high school. For *Granny Mo Bucks,* when she used to be heavy on Vine with Collin, making his friends and mine laugh. Shit like that made it hard for me to process. How a person can be here one day and gone the next. Death was inevitable, but it was also something that rarely crossed your mind when you didn't think your number was close to being called. And yeah, Granny had been hospitalized last year and a couple weeks before she passed... I still didn't want to think this was it.

"You need a moment?" Amani was watching me as I shook my head, quickly, knowing she didn't buy it as I chuckled softly. "We can take Dot to the back and sit," she suggested as I shook my head. "You sure?"

"Yeah, I'm good, Shawty," I told her after exhaling, pulling her into me for a kiss. "Eh, you chill out," I quickly got Dot together as she let out a small yelp.

"*She* is beautiful!" Marissa, my mama's old friend from college stopped in front of me gushing over Dot as my face tightened from the pride displayed on my face through my smile. "I didn't know you two had another baby!" Marissa exclaimed as she pulled Amani into a big, rocking hug.

"Yeah..." I bashfully skipped over the fact that she mistook Amani as Cairo's mama, too. "We ain't have nothin' to do last summer so I thought dis would speed things up—"

"Shut up!" Amani quickly slapped the back of her hand to my chest as me, Collin, and Marissa laughed.

"Men, right?" Marissa giggled as Amani rolled her eyes while nodding her head. "*Uh*—How old?"

"Two weeks—"

"*Two weeks?*" Marissa shrieked like everybody else had, at this repast after we told them Dot's age. "She shouldn't be out—"

"She'll be fine," Amani was quick to shut down anybody who thought she and I were risking a lot by bringing Dot out so early after birth. "It's just for the day and we'll be back home... Plus, Daddy's making sure nobody touches her," Amani assured Marissa who didn't know how to take my wife's response.

"Oh," was all she could say.

"Yeah... I'm on my job," I added as a buffer in case Marissa could sense the slight agitation in Amani's tone.

Shawty was a firecracker, low-key when she wanted to be. I'd learned early on not to fuck with her too much. Mani had two sides... Super silly or real serious and this was one of those moments when she'd spit fire if she felt she was being tested.

"I see..." Marissa got the underline meaning of what Amani was trying to convey and it got real awkward. "Well, it's nice seeing you again, *Carter*—Congrats on the new bundle and my condolences to you all," she bowed out quickly, making her way over to Collin who was smirking, overhearing everything as he hugged her.

Placing my left hand to the small of Amani's back she instantly looked up at me twisting her lips like she was innocent in the matter. Smirking and shaking my head, I kissed the top of her head to let her know I wasn't mad at how she handled things.

"She tried not to acknowledge you after you gathered dem edges, lil sis," Collin didn't make matters better as he leaned over to whisper to Amani as she giggled and shrugged. "I heard you got hands, so I was thinkin', maybe you and Eb—"

"Shut up, Lin," Ebony pinched him as we laughed.

"I'm just sayin—Marissa rolled up on da fam like she got it like dat... She ain't mama's real friend—"

"Shut yo ass up—*Silly muhfucka*," I grinned as Ebony, Amani, and Collin chuckled.

"Mani bossed up, like, *She'll be fine, bitch!*"

"I did not!" Amani giggled as a few eyes in the lineup looked over at us laughing.

"Now I see whatchu mean, bro—"

"What *do* you mean?" Amani quickly interjected as I glared over at Collin who was smirking and shrugging.

"*Tsk! Say,* Shawty, I ain't neva told him shit—"

"Hoe ass," Collin laughed with me.

"Quit playin' man—I got da baby in my hands—"

"Nah, beat his ass, lil sis!" Collin egged Amani on as we all laughed.

"Dis why I ain't wanna stand by yo ass," I mumbled as Collin laughed. "You need to go stand by yo mama so she can keep yo goofy ass in line."

"Nah, I'm good right here, *nigga*, where I need to be!"

"I don't know who's more annoying—"

"Clearly it's him," I cut Ebony off as Collin's face scrunched up to show he disagreed.

"On my mama, dat ain't me!" Collin puffed his chest out at Ebony as she giggled, pushing him away.

"On who?" My mama spoke getting all our attention. "Don't put nothing on me!" she told Collin as we laughed at him.

"*Tsk!* Ma, you ain't no fun!" Collin groaned, making everybody laugh even harder at him.

"Is that everybody?" My daddy asked my mama as she nodded, shrugging.

"I guess—I don't see anyone else," she was now looking towards her sisters as they shrugged too. "I guess we can eat—"

"Good!" Collin cheered as he broke from the line, taking Ebony's hand and dragging her with him. "Granny D wouldn't won't me to starve," he had no class but his ass was always funny.

Honestly, Collin was probably the most like Granny. He said what he wanted with no care of how you felt. But his words were never malice, despite not always thinking before he said them. Maybe a little more uncaring, than Granny, they both came from the same place—Humor. Always down for a good time and to keep everybody around them happy. *So, I guess I ain't fully lose my Granny.... She lives on through my brother.*

"You wanna come with me to change, Dot?" Amani asked, pulling me from my thoughts as I nodded my head. "Hey, Cai, do you mind saving *us* a seat?"

"Already on it!" Cairo held the diaper bag up for Amani to grabbed as he ran chased behind my mama.

Taking Amani's hand into mine, I couldn't take my eyes off her. More than ever before, she was now the image I'd seen of her in my head the first night I saw her in the club. Different from most, I read her vibe instantly. She smoked, so I was down, but when she spoke you knew she was well versed on many topics. Even after having sex on the first night, I didn't get a bad vibe from her. Yeah, a little crazy but she was going through something, at the time... And I just felt obligated to help her figure it out. Sweet as pie, Amani just had a softness about her, she glowed a little. You could tell she would do anything to make sure you were straight and even when her timid side snuck up, that little girl it transformed her into was just as gentle and meek.

"What?" Amani giggled as we made it into the dining hall's bathroom.

"Just thinkin'—"

"About?" Amani asked as she took Dot from my arms.

"You."

Blushing, Amani's eyes batted, but she never looked up from our daughter.

"You ain't gon' ask why?"

"I didn't think I had to but why?"

"Cuz you did make my dreams come true," I winked down at her as she smiled, trying not to show the red in her cheeks by covering them with her hands.

"Stop it—"

"Nah, you stop!" I poked her right hand as she lowered it to keep Dot still. "Sexy ass—"

"You better stop!" Amani pointed her left finger at me. "We are not in the type of place where you wanna be saying these kinds of things to me."

"Aw yeah... Wuss gon' happen if I don't?" I pushed up against her, careful not to move her hand from Dot as she giggled.

"Carter—Not in front of the baby," she giggled again, as Dot sighed, like she was over it already. "See, even Dot knows how much of a horny toad you are—"

"She should know—Shit," I smacked my lips causing Amani to laugh. "How she think she got here!"

"From the stork—"

"Da fuck it ain't—Quit playin' wit me, Mani... Dis my seed!" I slapped my palm against my chest proudly. "You see da resemblance—"

"I know... I had no parts," Amani groaned as she unsnapped Dot's bodysuit. "And that's probably how this thing is gonna go for the rest of our lives, *huh?*" She asked me as I nodded my head. "Go figure."

Wrapping my arms around her waist and kissing her cheek, Amani nestled the side of her face into my lips as she smiled.

"*Buck up Buttercup,*" I whispered in her ear as her laughter bounced off the walls. "Dis whatchu signed up for—*Cuz you got dat butta love, baybeh!*"

THE END!

GRADUATION DAY (EPILOGUE)

Amani

FEELING THE PALMS OF MY HANDS SWEATING, anticipation was steady building as the next name closest to mine had been called. No matter how much I tried psyching myself up, I couldn't shake my crowd-induced anxiety. *You wanted this, Amani, now get it together!* I told myself as I looked back at the crowd, focusing near the center where Carter, Cairo, Dot, and the rest of his family was located. They'd been screaming since my class walked out and their joy somewhat eased my nerves and doubled my anxiety. At the same time I was excited to have them here, I didn't want to trip or do anything remotely close to embarrassing in front of them, either. *God why did I marry a man with the last name Banks?* I could cry because I was so close to the top of the list, I could feel the announcer itching to call—

"Aman Monroe Banks—"

"THAT'S MY LADYEEEE! THAT'S MY LADYEHHHH!" I could hear Carter's loud voice seemingly over the crowd as the attention went from me to him.

Gladly, I accepted their laughter because most of them were doing what everybody did when Carter would bellow out a song in public... Cheer him on and sing right along with it. Clapping their hands and stomping, in sync, this graduation turned into an impromptu D'Angelo concert. All thanks to my husband.

"You're my little baybeh—"
"Baybeh!"
"My darlin' baybeh!"
"Baybeh!"
"Mani you're da talk of da town—And everybody wanna know wuss goin' down!"

Shielding my face as I grabbed my degree, I almost missed a couple hands to shake and my picture being taken because Carter and his choir had me blushing. The stomach flutters from earlier vanished from all the laughing and smiling I was doing as I walked across the stage.

"Congratulations, Amani, you did it," Dean Morrison hugged me, rocking back and forth like Mama Megan loved to do when she embraced me.

This must be a southern thing but I loved it. All the warmth and love you felt during this moment was just what you didn't think you needed.

"I know I'll see you back here for your masters!" She pointed as I nodded my head. "You go girl—Don't let nothing stop you from reaching your goals..." She giggled looking into the stands. "Even that silly husband of yours!" She cackled with me.

"This is my life," I smirked as she laughed some more.

"Enjoy it—"

"Oh, you don't have to tell me twice!" I called over my shoulder, "I love that crazy man!"

And I did. Probably said this so many times since I met him but I wouldn't trade being with Carter for no one in this world. Not Brandon, not anybody. And my sister told me how Brandon came to their house looking for me... I'm so glad she kept that from me until now. Probably wouldn't have gone chasing up behind him but now, after a whole year of living with Carter and the family we created together, I no longer felt anything in my heart for Brandon. Not even sympathy. He can stay in New Orleans and die there... Okay, maybe not die but he can stay out of my way. *I's a married woman, now!*

AMANI'S DAY (EPILOGUE)

Carter

With Dot in my arms and Cairo to my right holding the balloons and gift bag he'd picked out for Amani, we cheered loudly as she walked towards us. Her gown was unzipped, revealing the orange dress she wore underneath it to go with her blue gown, showcasing her school pride through wearing their colors.

"Look at my baby—Graduatin' and shit!" I chuckled pulling Amani into a hug. "We proud of you baby," I pecked her lips as she smiled, looking around me to see my family standing behind us.

"We truly are," my mama was next to hug Amani as Cairo

looked up torn. "I'm sorry Roro, I just jumped in front of you," she quickly apologized to Cairo while backing away from Amani to let him hug her.

"I gotchu a gift—I picked everything out myself," Cairo told Amani as she beamed, taking the bag and balloons from his hands. "Don't open it until we get in da car," he warned as Amani quickly closed the bag, nodding her head up and down.

"Okay, baby," she gripped Cairo's chin before kissed his cheek and hugging him a second time.

"Damn, must be nice," I mumbled causing Amani to giggled as she cut her eyes over at me.

"Do not even..." she smirked. "You're always getting something from me—"

"Alright now," my mama picked up on what she thought was an explicit conversation but it was far from the subject.

Now had I said it, yeah... I'd be talking about the real thing but I knew Amani's mind wasn't in the gutter half as much as mine was. Snickering as I pointed my finger, teasingly in her direction, my mama swatted at my hand to get me to stop an Amani pettily giggled, too.

"Congrats, Grad!" Ebony hugged Amani, holding just as many balloons as Cairo had when we got here and her two gift bags for her. "It's not baby stuff, I promise," Ebony told Amani who squinted her eyes like she had x-ray vision before laughing.

"I hope not—Dot has way too much, already," she exhaled as I groaned loud enough for everybody to hear. "Don't even say it!" Amani held up her palm because she already knew what I was gonna say before I opened my mouth.

Grinning and smacking my lips, Amani continued to hug and receive gifts from the rest of my family as a few of her classmates walked up to her for pictures and even more hugs. Seeing Amani in her studious element did something to me. I mean, I knew my wife was smart but watching her flow through the sea of people, hugging and retelling little stories from the semester put a smile on my face.

"Call me when you get home," Shanae hugged Amani again before turning towards Dot to pinch her cheeks. "I'll see you tomorrow, pretty girl—Bye Carter and Cairo!"

"Bye, Shanae!" Cairo called out while waving.

"Bye, Shanae," I followed up as she walked back to her family.

"So, when am I getting my wedding?"

Groaning as I side eyed my mama, I could hear my father chuckling. I see, now, my Mama wasn't gonna drop this shit until she had a date set. Looking down at Amani, her shoulders were half raised as the perplexed look on her face let me know, I'd have to toss a day out and hope we had shit ready then.

"I'on know..." I shrugged as my mama's scowl deepened. "Fix ya face, *woman*... We'll do dis shit around Mother's Day—"

"*Mother's Day?*" she exclaimed as I smacked my lips causing me to huff.

"Mama dat shit like four weeks away," Collin chimed in laughing.

"For real—"

"Don't tag team me," my mama pointed towards Collin as she rolled her eyes. "I've already waited too long—"

"You act like we wasn't goin' through a lot, already, ma!"

If it sounded like I was whining, I was, lowkey. And only my mama could bring this side out of me.

"Granny passed, Mani had da baby—She just graduated," I shot out three important events a wedding would've been too much for.

"The boy's right, Meg," my daddy finally spoke up as the tight look on my mama's face softened. "He and Mani have to settle down a little more—Then I'm sure they'll be open to planning and whatever else."

"Yeah," I added in knowing it would annoy my mama and make everybody else laugh.

Catching her glare and Amani's head shaking had me laughing harder than anyone else.

"We good now?" Collin asked looking off to the side, rubbing his stomach.

Nobody answered at first but that was a sign that my mama would drop this wedding talk for now. And that's all I wanted, right now. Today was Mani's day. She got her degree, and we still had a little bit of sun and the whole night to celebrate her.

"Y'all down for some Plucker's?" I asked as Collin's eyes lit up with his posture.

"Hell yeah—I just told you I wanted some wings," he tapped Ebony who was smiling and nodding. "*Manganero* and *Spicy Lemon Pepper*..." My lil brother clasped his hands together before rubbing them together.

"Pluckers it is!" I confirmed with the family, getting head nods and murmuring. "C'mon—I bet half da people here finna try to head dat way," I quickly grabbed Amani by the hand as we all raced to our individual rides.

Putting Dot in her seat, baby girl was officially a full month and putting on weight. Chunky with the rolls to match, she'd replaced her mother as my cuddle buddy. On the couch, my bed, anywhere we were together, Dot was in my arms, taking up space. Amani liked to pretend like it didn't bother her but I've caught her more than a few times just staring as I showered Dot with kisses, in the middle of my shows. Shawty ain't have nothing to worry about, though, because she was always gonna be my number one lady. Dot just my baby, right now.

"I'm really proud of you, Shawty," I told Amani again after we were buckled up and ready to go.

"Thank you and thank you, again because all that pushing and making sure I stuck to my guns kept me from just blowing it off," Amani told me as I nodded once, starting the truck up. "You'd made my dreams come true, too," she told me as I intertwined our fingers together, kissing the back of her hand.

"I know... Dats my job," I winked at her and watched her cheeks flush.

Backing out my spot, I hit the bluetooth button and turned the volume dial. Today was gonna be like every day... *Good!*

> *Get a bag, yeah that's when the woes come*
> *Throw it back, keep that ass in motion*
> *Aw you mad, you must think I owe you something*
> *Bitch act like you know something...*

IF YOU WANT TO CONTINUE THEIR STORY... CLICK HERE.

OTHERWISE...

The End

ABOUT THE AUTHOR

Käixo is the author of multiple urban fiction series and books. She began writing at the tender age of six and hasn't stopped since. Continuing her passion for writing, Käixo and her daughter reside in her hometown of Chicago.